J.B. Nichols and Sons

A Lamport garland from the library of Sir Charles Edmund Isham,

Bart.

Comprising four unique works hitherto unknown

J.B. Nichols and Sons

A Lamport garland from the library of Sir Charles Edmund Isham, Bart.
Comprising four unique works hitherto unknown

ISBN/EAN: 9783742870063

Manufactured in Europe, USA, Canada, Australia, Japa

Cover: Foto ©Andreas Hilbeck / pixelio.de

Manufactured and distributed by brebook publishing software
(www.brebook.com)

J.B. Nichols and Sons

A Lamport garland from the library of Sir Charles Edmund Isham,

Bart.

A

LAMPORT GARLAND

FROM THE LIBRARY

OF

SIR CHARLES EDMUND ISHAM, BART

COMPRISING

FOUR UNIQUE WORKS

HITHERTO UNKNOWN.

PRINTED FOR THE

Roxburghe Club.

LONDON:
J. B. NICHOLS AND SONS, 25, PARLIAMENT STREET.

MDCCCLXXXI.

A LAMPORT GARLAND.

Roxburghe Club.

The Roxburghe Club.

MDCCCLXXXII.

THE DUKE OF BUCCLEUCH AND QUEENSBERRY, K.G.

PRESIDENT.

MARQUIS OF LOTHIAN.
MARQUIS OF BATH.
EARL OF CRAWFORD.
EARL OF CARNARVON.
EARL OF POWIS, *V.P.*
EARL BEAUCHAMP.
EARL OF CAWDOR.
LORD ZOUCHE.
LORD HOUGHTON.
LORD COLERIDGE.
BARON HEATH.
RIGHT HON. ALEX. JAMES BERESFORD HOPE.
SIR WILLIAM REYNELL ANSON, BART.
SIR EDWARD HULSE, BART.
ARTHUR JAMES BALFOUR, ESQ
HENRY BRADSHAW, ESQ.
HENRY ARTHUR BRIGHT, ESQ.
REV. WILLIAM EDWARD BUCKLEY.

FRANCIS HENRY DICKINSON, ESQ.
GEORGE BRISCOE EYRE, ESQ.
THOMAS GAISFORD, ESQ.
HENRY HUCKS GIBBS, ESQ. *Treasurer.*
ALBAN GEORGE HENRY GIBBS, ESQ.
RALPH NEVILLE GRENVILLE, ESQ.
ROBERT STAYNER HOLFORD, ESQ.
JOHN MALCOLM, ESQ.
JOHN COLE NICHOLL, ESQ.
EVELYN PHILIP SHIRLEY, ESQ.
EDWARD JAMES STANLEY, ESQ.
SIMON WATSON TAYLOR, ESQ.
REV. WILLIAM HEPWORTH THOMPSON, D.D.
GEORGE TOMLINE, ESQ.
REV. EDWARD TINDAL TURNER.
VICTOR WILLIAM BATES VAN DE WEYER, ESQ.
W. ALDIS WRIGHT, ESQ.

Roxburghe Club.

1812. PRESIDENT.

1. GEORGE JOHN, EARL SPENCER.

1812.	2.	WILLIAM SPENCER, DUKE OF DEVONSHIRE.
1812.	3	GEORGE SPENCER CHURCHILL, MARQUIS OF BLANDFORD.
		1817. DUKE OF MARLBOROUGH.
1812.	4.	GEORGE GRANVILLE LEVESON GOWER, EARL GOWER.
		1833. MARQUIS OF STAFFORD.
		1833. DUKE OF SUTHERLAND.
1812.	5.	GEORGE HOWARD, VISCOUNT MORPETH.
		1825. EARL OF CARLISLE.
1812.	6.	JOHN CHARLES SPENCER, VISCOUNT ALTHORP.
		1834. EARL SPENCER.
1812.	7.	SIR MARK MASTERMAN SYKES, BART.
1812.	8.	SIR SAMUEL EGERTON BRYDGES, BART.
1812.	9.	WILLIAM BENTHAM, ESQ.
1812.	10.	WILLIAM BOLLAND, ESQ.
		1829. SIR WILLIAM BOLLAND. KNT.
1812.	11.	JAMES BOSWELL, ESQ.
1812.	12.	REV. WILLIAM HOLWELL CARR.
1812.	13.	JOHN DENT. ESQ.
1812.	14	REV. THOMAS FROGNALL DIBDIN.
1812.	15.	REV. HENRY DRURY.

1812.	16.	FRANCIS FREELING, ESQ.
		1828. SIR FRANCIS FREELING, BART.
1812.	17.	GEORGE HENRY FREELING, ESQ.
		1836. SIR GEORGE HENRY FREELING, BART.
1812.	18.	JOSEPH HASLEWOOD, ESQ.
1812.	19.	RICHARD HEBER, ESQ.
1812.	20.	REV. THOMAS CUTHBERT HEBER.
1812.	21.	GEORGE ISTED, ESQ.
1812.	22.	ROBERT LANG, ESQ.
1812.	23.	JOSEPH LITTLEDALE, ESQ.
		1824. SIR JOSEPH LITTLEDALE, KNT.
1812.	24.	JAMES HEYWOOD MARKLAND, ESQ.
1812.	25.	JOHN DELAFIELD PHELPS, ESQ.
1812.	26.	THOMAS PONTON, ESQ.
1812.	27.	PEREGRINE TOWNELEY, ESQ.
1812.	28.	EDWARD VERNON UTTERSON, ESQ.
1812.	29.	ROGER WILBRAHAM, ESQ.
1812.	30.	REV. JAMES WILLIAM DODD.
1812.	31.	EDWARD LITTLEDALE, ESQ.

1816.	32.	GEORGE HIBBERT, ESQ.
1819.	33.	SIR ALEXANDER BOSWELL, BART.
1822.	34.	GEORGE WATSON TAYLOR, ESQ.
1822.	35.	JOHN ARTHUR LLOYD, ESQ.
1822.	36.	VENERABLE ARCHDEACON WRANGHAM.
1823.	37.	THE AUTHOR OF WAVERLEY.
		1827. SIR WALTER SCOTT, BART.
1827.	38.	HON. AND REV. GEORGE NEVILLE GRENVILLE.
		1846. DEAN OF WINDSOR.
1828.	39.	EDWARD HERBERT, VISCOUNT CLIVE.
		1839. EARL OF POWIS.
1830.	40.	JOHN FREDERICK, EARL OF CAWDOR.
1831.	41.	REV. EDWARD CRAVEN HAWTREY, D.D.
1834.	42.	SIR STEPHEN RICHARD GLYNNE, BART.
1834.	43.	BENJAMIN BARNARD, ESQ.
1834.	44.	VENERABLE ARCHDEACON BUTLER, D.D.
		1836. SAMUEL, LORD BISHOP OF LICHFIELD.

1835. PRESIDENT.

EDWARD HERBERT, VISCOUNT CLIVE.

1839. EARL OF POWIS.

1835.	45.	WALTER FRANCIS, DUKE OF BUCCLEUCH AND QUEENSBERRY.
1836.	46.	RIGHT HONOURABLE LORD FRANCIS EGERTON.
		1846. EARL OF ELLESMERE.
1836.	47.	ARCHIBALD ACHESON, VISCOUNT ACHESON.
		1849. EARL OF GOSFORD.
1836.	48.	BERIAH BOTFIELD, ESQ.
1836.	49.	HENRY HALLAM, ESQ.
1837.	50.	PHILIP HENRY STANHOPE, VISCOUNT MAHON.
		1855. EARL STANHOPE.
1838.	51.	GEORGE JOHN, LORD VERNON.
1838.	52.	REV. PHILIP BLISS, D.C.L.
1839.	53.	RIGHT HONOURABLE SIR JAMES PARKE, KNT.
		1856. LORD WENSLEYDALE.
1839.	54.	REV. BULKELEY BANDINEL, D.D.
1839.	55.	WILLIAM HENRY MILLER, ESQ.
1839.	56.	EVELYN PHILIP SHIRLEY, ESQ.
1840.	57.	EDWARD JAMES HERBERT, VISCOUNT CLIVE.
		1848. EARL OF POWIS.
1841.	58.	DAVID DUNDAS, ESQ.
		1847. SIR DAVID DUNDAS, KNT.
1842.	59.	JOHN EARL BROWNLOW.
1842.	60.	HONOURABLE HUGH CHOLMONDELEY.
		1855. LORD DELAMERE.
1844.	61.	SIR ROBERT HARRY INGLIS, BART.
1844.	62.	ALEXANDER JAMES BERESFORD HOPE, ESQ.
1844.	63.	REV. HENRY WELLESLEY.
1845.	64.	ANDREW RUTHERFURD, ESQ.
		1851. LORD RUTHERFURD.
1846.	65.	HON. ROBERT CURZON, JUN.
1846.	66.	GEORGE TOMLINE, ESQ.
1846.	67.	WILLIAM STIRLING, ESQ.
		1866. SIR WILLIAM STIRLING MAXWELL, BART.
1847.	68.	FRANCIS HENRY DICKINSON, ESQ.

WALTER FRANCIS, DUKE OF BUCCLEUCH AND QUEENSBERRY, K.G.

1848.	69.	NATHANIEL BLAND, ESQ.
1848.	70.	REV. WILLIAM EDWARD BUCKLEY.
1849	71.	REV. JOHN STUART HIPPISLEY HORNER.
1849.	72.	HIS EXCELLENCY MONSIEUR VAN DE WEYER.
1849.	73.	MELVILLE PORTAL, ESQ.
1851.	74.	ROBERT STAYNER HOLFORD, ESQ.
	75.	PAUL BUTLER, ESQ.
	76.	EDWARD HULSE, ESQ.
		1855. SIR EDWARD HULSE, BART.
1853.	77.	CHARLES TOWNELEY, ESQ.
1854.	78.	WILLIAM ALEX. ANTH. ARCH. DUKE OF HAMILTON AND BRANDON.
	79.	HENRY HOWARD MOLYNEUX, EARL OF CARNARVON.
1855.	80.	SIR JOHN BENN WALSH, BART.
		1868. LORD ORMATHWAITE.
	81.	ADRIAN JOHN HOPE, ESQ.
	82.	RALPH NEVILLE GRENVILLE, ESQ.
1856.	83.	SIR JOHN SIMEON, BART.
	84.	SIR JAMES SHAW WILLES, KNT.
1857.	85.	GEORGE GRANVILLE FRANCIS, EARL OF ELLESMERE.
	86.	WILLIAM SCHOMBERG ROBERT, MARQUIS OF LOTHIAN.
	87.	FREDERICK TEMPLE, LORD DUFFERIN.
		1872. EARL OF DUFFERIN.
1858.	88.	SIMON WATSON TAYLOR, ESQ.
	89.	THOMAS GAISFORD, ESQ.
1861.	90.	JOHN FREDERICK VAUGHAN, EARL CAWDOR.
1863.	91.	GRANVILLE LEVESON GOWER, ESQ.
	92.	HENRY HUCKS GIBBS, ESQ.
1864.	93.	RICHARD MONCKTON, LORD HOUGHTON.
	94.	CHRISTOPHER SYKES, ESQ.
	95.	REV. HENRY OCTAVIUS COXE.
	96.	REV. WILLIAM GEORGE CLARK.
	97.	REV. CHARLES HENRY HARTSHORNE.
	98.	JOHN COLE NICHOLL, ESQ.
	99.	GEORGE BRISCOE EYRE, ESQ.
	100.	JOHN BENJAMIN HEATH, ESQ.
1866.	101.	HENRY HUTH, ES .
	102.	HENRY BRADSHAW, ESQ.
1867.	103.	FREDERICK, EARL BEAUCHAMP.
	104.	KIRKMAN DANIEL HODGSON, ESQ.
1868.	105.	CHARLES WYNNE FINCH, ESQ.

Roxburghe Club.

CATALOGUE OF THE BOOKS

PRESENTED TO

AND PRINTED BY THE CLUB.

LONDON:

MDCCCLXXXII.

CATALOGUE.

Certaine Bokes of VIRGILES Aenaeis, turned into English Meter. By the Right Honorable Lorde, HENRY EARLE OF SURREY.

> WILLIAM BOLLAND, ESQ. 1814.

Caltha Poetarum; or, The Bumble Bee. By T. CUTWODE, ESQ.

> RICHARD HEBER, ESQ. 1815.

The Three First Books of OVID de Tristibus, Translated into English. By THOMAS CHURCHYARDE.

> EARL SPENCER, PRESIDENT. 1816.

Poems. By RICHARD BARNFIELD.

> JAMES BOSWELL, ESQ. 1816.

DOLARNEY'S Primerose or the First part of the Passionate Hermit.

> SIR FRANCIS FREELING, BART. 1816.

La Contenance de la Table.

> GEORGE HENRY FREELING, ESQ. 1816.

Newes from Scotland, declaring the Damnable Life of Doctor Fian, a notable Sorcerer, who was burned at Edenbrough in Ianuarie last 1591.

> GEORGE HENRY FREELING, ESQ. 1816.

A proper new Interlude of the World and the Child, otherwise called Mundus et Infans.

> VISCOUNT ALTHORP. 1817.

HAGTHORPE Revived; or Select Specimens of a Forgotten Poet.

> SIR SAMUEL EGERTON BRYDGES, BART. 1817.

4

Istoria novellamente ritrovata di due nobili **Amanti**, &c. da Luigi Porto.

Rev. William Holwell Carr. 1817.

The Funeralles of King Edward the Sixt.

Rev. James William Dodd. 1817.

A Roxburghe Garland, 12mo.

James Boswell, Esq. 1817.

Cock Lorell's Boat, a Fragment from the original in the British Museum.

Rev. Henry Drury. 1817.

Le Livre du Faucon.

Robert Lang, Esq. 1817.

The Glutton's Feaver. By Thomas Bancroft.

John Delafield Phelps, Esq. 1817.

The Chorle and the Birde.

Sir Mark Masterman Sykes, Bart. 1818.

Daiphantus, or the Passions of Love. By Antony Scoloker.

Roger Wilbraham, Esq. 1818.

The Complaint of a Lover's Life.
Controversy between a Lover and a Jay.

Rev. Thomas Frognall Dibdin, Vice President. 1818.

Balades and other Poems. By John Gower. Printed from the original Manuscript in the Library of the Marquis of Stafford, at Trentham.

Earl Gower. 1818.

Diana; or the excellent conceitful Sonnets of H. C., supposed to have been printed either in 1592 or 1594.

Edward Littledale, Esq. 1818.

Chester Mysteries. De Deluvio Noe. De Occisione Innocentium.

James Heywood Markland, Esq. 1818.

Ceremonial at the Marriage of Mary Queen of Scotts with the Dauphin of France.

WILLIAM BENTHAM, ESQ. 1818.

The Solempnities and Triumphes doon and made at the Spousells and Marriage of the King's Daughter the Ladye Marye to the Prynce of Castile, Archduke of Austrige.

JOHN DENT, ESQ. 1818.

The Life of St. Ursula.
Guiscard and Sigismund.

DUKE OF DEVONSHIRE. 1818.

Le Morte Arthur. The Adventures of Sir Launcelot Du Lake.

THOMAS PONTON, ESQ. 1819.

Six Bookes of Metamorphoseos in whyche ben conteyned the Fables of OVYDE. Translated out of Frensshe into Englysshe by WILLIAM CAXTON. Printed from a Manuscript in the Library of Mr. Secretary Pepys, in the College of St. Mary Magdalen, in the University of Cambridge.

GEORGE HIBBERT, ESQ. 1819.

Chevelere Assigne.

EDWARD VERNON UTTERSON, ESQ. 1820.

Two Interludes : Jack Jugler and Thersytes.

JOSEPH HASLEWOOD, ESQ. 1820.

The New Notborune Mayd. The Boke of Mayd Emlyn.

GEORGE ISTED, ESQ. 1820.

The Book of Life ; a Bibliographical Melody.
Dedicated to the Roxburghe Club by RICHARD THOMSON.

8vo. 1820.

Magnyfycence : an Interlude. By JOHN SKELTON, Poet Laureat to Henry VIII.

JOSEPH LITTLEDALE, ESQ. 1821.

Judicium, a Pageant. Extracted from the Towneley Manuscript of Ancient Mysteries.

PEREGRINE EDWARD TOWNELEY, ESQ. 1822.

An Elegiacal Poem, on the Death of Thomas Lord Grey, of Wilton. By ROBERT MARSTON. From a Manuscript in the Library of The Right Honourable Thomas Grenville.

VISCOUNT MORPETH. 1822.

Selections from the Works of THOMAS RAVENSCROFT; a Musical Composer of the time of King James the First.

DUKE OF MARLBOROUGH. 1822.

LÆLII PEREGRINI Oratio in Obitum Torquati Tassi. Editio secunda.

SIR SAMUEL EGERTON BRYDGES, BART. 1822.

The Hors, the Shepe, and the Ghoos.

SIR MARK MASTERMAN SYKES, BART. 1822.

The Metrical Life of Saint Robert of Knaresborough.

REV. HENRY DRURY. 1824.

Informacōn for Pylgrymes unto the Holy Londe. From a rare Tract in the Library of the Faculty of Advocates, Edinburgh.

GEORGE HENRY FREELING, ESQ. 1824.

The Cuck-Queanes and Cuckolds Errants or the Bearing Down the Inne, a Comædie. The Faery Pastorall or Forrest of Elues. By W—— P——, Esq.

JOHN ARTHUR LLOYD, ESQ. 1824.

The Garden Plot, an Allegorical Poem, inscribed to Queen Elizabeth. By HENRY GOLDINGHAM. From an unpublished Manuscript of the Harleian Collection in the British Museum. To which are added some account of the Author; also a reprint of his Masques performed before the Queen at Norwich on Thursday, August 21, 1578.

VENERABLE ARCHDEACON WRANGHAM. 1825.

La Rotta de Francciosi a Terroana novamente facta.
La Rotta de Scocesi.

EARL SPENCER, PRESIDENT.   1825.

Nouvelle Edition d'un Poeme sur la Journée de Guinegate.
Presented by the MARQUIS DE FORTIA.   1825.

Zuléima, par C. PICHLER.   12mo.
Presented by H. DE CHATEAUGIRON.   1825.

Poems, written in English, by CHARLES DUKE OF ORLEANS, during
his Captivity in England after the Battle of Azincourt.

GEORGE WATSON TAYLOR, ESQ.   1827.

Proceedings in the Court Martial held upon John, Master of
Sinclair, Captain-Lieutenant in Preston's Regiment, for the
Murder of Ensign Schaw of the same Regiment, and Captain
Schaw, of the Royals, 17 October, 1708; with Correspondence
respecting that Transaction.

SIR WALTER SCOTT, BART.   1828.

The Ancient English Romance of Havelok the Dane; accompanied
by the French Text: with an Introduction, Notes, and a
Glossary.   By FREDERIC MADDEN, ESQ.

PRINTED FOR THE CLUB.   1828.

GAUFRIDI ARTHURII MONEMUTHENSIS Archidiaconi, postea vero
Episcopi Asaphensis, de Vita et Vaticiniis Merlini Calidonii,
Carmen Heroicum.

HON. and REV. G. NEVILLE GRENVILLE.   1830.

The Ancient English Romance of William and the Werwolf; edited
from an unique copy in King's College Library, Cambridge;
with an Introduction and Glossary.   By FREDERIC MADDEN
Esq.

EARL CAWDOR.   1832.

The Private Diary of WILLIAM, first EARL COWPER, Lord Chancellor of England.

> REV. EDWARD CRAVEN HAWTREY.   1833.

The Lyvys of Seyntes; translated into Englys be a Doctour of Dyuynite clepyd OSBERN BOKENAM, frer Austyn of the Convent of Stocklare.

> VISCOUNT CLIVE, PRESIDENT.   1835.

A Little Boke of Ballads.

> Dedicated to the Club by E. V. UTTERSON, ESQ.   1836.

The Love of Wales to their Soueraigne Prince, expressed in a true Relation of the Solemnity held at Ludlow, in the Countie of Salop, upon the fourth of November last past, Anno Domini 1616, being the day of the Creation of the high and mighty Charles, Prince of Wales, and Earle of Chester, in his Maiesties Palace of White-Hall.

> Presented by the HONOURABLE R. H. CLIVE.   1837.

Sidneiana, being a collection of Fragments relative to Sir Philip Sidney, Knight, and his immediate Connexions.

> BISHOP OF LICHFIELD.   1837.

The Owl and the Nightingale, a Poem of the Twelfth Century. Now first printed from Manuscripts in the Cottonian Library, and at Jesus' College, Oxford; with an Introduction and Glossary.   Edited by JOSEPHUS STEVENSON, ESQ.

> SIR STEPHEN RICHARD GLYNNE, BART.   1838.

The Old English Version of the Gesta Romanorum : edited for the first time from Manuscripts in the British Museum and University Library, Cambridge, with an Introduction and Notes, by SIR FREDERIC MADDEN, K.H.

> PRINTED FOR THE CLUB.   1838.

Illustrations of Ancient State and Chivalry, from MSS. preserved in the Ashmolean Museum, with an Appendix.

> BENJAMIN BARNARD, ESQ. 1840.

Manners and Household Expenses of England in the Thirteenth and Fifteenth Centuries, illustrated by original Records. I. Household Roll of Eleanor Countess of Leicester, A.D. 1265. II. Accounts of the Executors of Eleanor Queen Consort of Edward I. A.D. 1291. III. Accounts and Memoranda of Sir John Howard, first Duke of Norfolk, A.D. 1462 to A.D. 1471.

> BERIAH BOTFIELD, ESQ. 1841.

The Black Prince, an Historical Poem, written in French, by CHANDOS HERALD; with a Translation and Notes by the Rev. HENRY OCTAVIUS COXE, M.A.

> PRINTED FOR THE CLUB. 1842.

The Decline of the last Stuarts. Extracts from the Despatches of British Envoys to the Secretary of State.

> PRINTED FOR THE CLUB. 1843.

Vox Populi Vox Dei, a Complaynt of the Comons against Taxes. Presented according to the Direction of the late

> RIGHT HON. SIR JOSEPH LITTLEDALE, KNT. 1843.

Household Books of John Duke of Norfolk and Thomas Earl of Surrey; temp. 1481—1490. From the original Manuscripts in the Library of the Society of Antiquaries, London. Edited by J. PAYNE COLLIER, ESQ., F.S.A.

> PRINTED FOR THE CLUB. 1844.

Three Collections of English Poetry of the latter part of the Sixteenth Century.

> Presented by the DUKE OF NORTHUMBERLAND, K.G. 1845.

Historical Papers, Part I. Castra Regia, a Treatise on the Succession to the Crown of England, addressed to Queen Elizabeth by ROGER EDWARDS, ESQ., in 1568. Novissima Straffordii. Some account of the Proceedings against, and Demeanor of, Thomas Wentworth, Earl of Strafford, both before and during his Trial, as well as at his Execution; written in Latin by ABRAHAM WRIGHT, Vicar of Okeham, in Rutlandshire. The same (endeauord) in English by JAMES WRIGHT, Barrister at Law.

REV. PHILIP BLISS, D.C.L., and REV. BULKELEY BANDINEL. 1846.

Correspondence of SIR HENRY UNTON, KNT., Ambassador from Queen Elizabeth to Henry IV. King of France, in the years MDXCI. and MDXCII. From the originals and authentic copies in the State Paper Office, the British Museum, and the Bodleian Library. Edited by the REV. JOSEPH STEVENSON, M.A.   PRINTED FOR THE CLUB. 1847.

La Vraie Cronicque d'Escoce. Pretensions des Anglois à la Couronne de France. Diplome de Jacques VI. Roi de la Grande Bretagne. Drawn from the Burgundian Library by Major Robert Anstruther.

PRINTED FOR THE CLUB. 1847.

The Sherley Brothers, an Historical Memoir of the Lives of Sir Thomas Sherley, Sir Anthony Sherley, and Sir Robert Sherley, Knights, by one of the same House. Edited and Presented by EVELYN PHILIP SHIRLEY, ESQ. 1848.

The Alliterative Romance of Alexander. From the unique Manuscript in the Ashmolean Museum. Edited by the REV. JOSEPH STEVENSON, M.A.

PRINTED FOR THE CLUB. 1849.

Letters and Dispatches from SIR HENRY WOTTON to James the First and his Ministers, in the years MDCXVII—XX. Printed from the originals in the Library of Eton College.

GEORGE TOMLINE, ESQ. 1850.

Poema quod dicitur Vox Clamantis, necnon Chronica Tripartita, auctore JOHANNE GOWER, nunc primum edidit H. O. COXE, M.A.   PRINTED FOR THE CLUB. 1850.

Five Old Plays. Edited from Copies, either unique or of great rarity, by J. PAYNE COLLIER, ESQ., F.S.A.

PRINTED FOR THE CLUB. 1851.

The Romaunce of the Sowdone of Babylone and of Ferumbras his Sone who conquerede Rome.

THE DUKE OF BUCCLEUCH, PRESIDENT. 1854.

The Ayenbite of Inwyt. From the Autograph MS. in the British Museum. Edited by the REV. JOSEPH STEVENSON, M.A.

PRINTED FOR THE CLUB. 1855.

John de Garlande, de Triumphis Ecclesiæ Libri Octo. A Latin Poem of the Thirteenth Century. Edited, from the unique Manuscript in the British Museum, by THOMAS WRIGHT, ESQ., M.A., F.S.A., Hon. M.R.S.L., &c. &c.

EARL OF POWIS. 1856.

Poems by MICHAEL DRAYTON. From the earliest and rarest Editions, or from Copies entirely unique. Edited, with Notes and Illustrations, and a new Memoir of the Author, by J. PAYNE COLLIER, ESQ., F.S.A.   PRINTED FOR THE CLUB. 1856.

Literary Remains of KING EDWARD THE SIXTH. In Two Volumes. Edited from his Autograph Manuscripts, with Historical Notes and a Biographical Memoir, by JOHN GOUGH NICHOLS, F.S.A.

PRINTED FOR THE CLUB. 1857.

The Itineraries of WILLIAM WEY, Fellow of Eton College, to Jerusalem, A.D. 1458 and A.D. 1462; and to Saint James of Compostella, A.D. 1456. From the Original MS. in the Bodleian Library. PRINTED FOR THE CLUB. 1857.

The Boke of Noblesse; Addressed to King Edward the Fourth on his Invasion of France in 1475. With an Introduction by JOHN GOUGH NICHOLS, F.S.A.

LORD DELAMERE. 1860.

Songs and Ballads, with other Short Poems, chiefly of the Reign of Philip and Mary. Edited, from a Manuscript in the Ashmolean Museum, by THOMAS WRIGHT, ESQ., M.A., F.S A., &c. &c.

ROBERT S. HOLFORD, ESQ. 1860.

De Regimine Principum, a Poem by THOMAS OCCLEVE, written in the Reign of Henry IV. Edited for the first time by THOMAS WRIGHT, ESQ., M.A., F.S.A., &c. &c.

PRINTED FOR THE CLUB. 1860.

The History of the Holy Graal; partly in English Verse by Henry Lonelich, Skynner, and wholly in French Prose by Sires Robiers de Borron. In two volumes. Edited, from MSS. in the Library of Corpus Christi College, Cambridge, and the British Museum, by FREDERICK J. FURNIVALL, ESQ., M.A., Trinity Hall, Cambridge.

PRINTED FOR THE CLUB. 1861 AND 1863.

Roberd of Brunne's Handlyng Synne, written A.D. 1203; with the French Treatise on which it is founded, Le Manuel des Pechies by William of Waddington. From MSS. in the British Museum and Bodleian Libraries. Edited by FREDERICK J. FURNIVALL, ESQ., M.A.

PRINTED FOR THE CLUB. 1862.

The Old English Version of Partonope of Blois. Edited for the first time from MSS. in University College Library and the Bodleian at Oxford, by the REV. W. E. BUCKLEY, M.A., Rector of Middleton Cheney, and formerly Fellow of Brasenose College.   PRINTED FOR THE CLUB.   1862.

Philosophaster, Comœdia; Poemata, auctore Roberto Burtono, S. Th. B., Democrito Juniore, Ex Æde Christi Oxon.
                    REV. WILLIAM EDWARD BUCKLEY.   1862.

La Queste del Saint Graal. In the French Prose of Maistres Gautiers Map, or Walter Map. Edited by FREDERICK J. FURNIVALL, Esq., M.A., Trinity Hall, Cambridge.
                         PRINTED FOR THE CLUB.   1864.

A Royal Historie of the excellent Knight Generides.
                         HENRY HUCKS GIBBS, ESQ.   1865.

The Copy-Book of Sir Amias Poulet's Letters, written during his Embassy in France, A.D. 1577.
                         PRINTED FOR THE CLUB.   1866.

The Bokes of Nurture and Kervynge.
                         HON. ROBERT CURZON.   1867.

A Map of the Holy Land, illustrating Wey's Itineraries.
                         PRINTED FOR THE CLUB.   1867.

Historia Quatuor Regum Angliæ, authore Johanne Herdo.
                         SIMON WATSON TAYLOR, ESQ.   1868.

Letters of Patrick Ruthven, Earl of Forth and Brentford, 1615—1662.   DUKE OF BUCCLEUCH, PRESIDENT.   1868.

The Pilgrimage of the Lyf of the Manhode, from the French of Guillaume de Deguileville.   PRINTED FOR THE CLUB.   1869.

Correspondence of Colonel N. Hooke, 1703—1707. Vol. I.
                         PRINTED FOR THE CLUB.   1870—1.

Liber Regalis; seu ordo Consecrandi Regem et Reginam.

EARL BEAUCHAMP. 1870.

Le Mystère de Saint Louis, Roi de France.

PRINTED FOR THE CLUB. 1871.

Correspondence of Colonel N. Hooke, 1703—1707. Vol. II.

PRINTED FOR THE CLUB. 1871.

The History of the Most Noble Knight Plasidas, and other Pieces; from the Pepysian Library. PRINTED FOR THE CLUB. 1873.

Florian and Florete, a Metrical Romance.

MARQUIS OF LOTHIAN. 1873.

A Fragment of Partonope of Blois, from a Manuscript at Vale Royal. PRINTED FOR THE CLUB. 1873.

The Legend of Sir Nicholas Throckmorton.

PAUL BUTLER, ESQ. 1874.

Correspondence of the First Earl of Ancram and the Third Earl of Lothian. 1616—1687. 2 Vols.

MARQUIS OF LOTHIAN. 1875.

The History of Grisild the Second.

JOHN BENJAMIN HEATH, ESQ. 1875.

The Complete Poems of Richard Barnfield.

PRINTED FOR THE CLUB. 1876.

The Apocalypse of St. John, from an Anglo-Saxon Manuscript.

PRINTED FOR THE CLUB. 1876.

Poems from Sir Kenelm Digby's Papers.

HENRY ARTHUR BRIGHT, ESQ. 1877.

Cephalus and Procris, by THOMAS EDWARDS.

PRINTED FOR THE CLUB. 1880—2.

Sir John Harington on the Succession to the Crown, 1602.

                        PRINTED FOR THE CLUB.   1880.

An Inquisition of the Manors of Glastonbury Abbey. 1589.

                        MARQUIS OF BATH. 1582.

The Lamport Garland.

                        PRINTED FOR THE CLUB.   1882.

TO THE READER.

The four Poetical Pieces, each unique, which conſtitute the preſent volume, were placed by Sir Charles Edmund Iſham, Baronet, of Lamport Hall, Northamptonſhire, at the diſpoſal of the Roxburghe Club for republication under the Editorial care of Mr. Charles Edmonds, by whom their exiſtence was firſt made known.

The ownerſhip and local habitation of theſe treaſures is intimated by the title "A Lamport Garland," with the ſhield of Sir Charles Iſham on the keyſtone of the arch. On the dexter and ſiniſter pillars are the ſhields of the Earl of Powis, Vice-Preſident, and Mr. H. H. Gibbs, Treaſurer, of the Roxburghe Club; beneath which reſpectively are thoſe of Mr. Gaisford and Mr. Buckley, Members of the Printing Committee, who were deputed to ſuperintend the progreſs of this volume through the preſs.

Engraved on a larger ſcale, and on a ſeparate leaf fronting the title-page, is the ſhield of His Grace the Duke of Buccleuch, Preſident of the Roxburghe Club :

Ο ΔΕ ΜΙΝ ΣΑΚΕΙ ΚΡΤΠΤΑΣΚΕ ΦΑΕΙΝΩΙ.

W. E. BUCKLEY.

T. GAISFORD.

ɪ

EDITOR'S NOTE.

The Editor thinks it neceſſary to ſtate that had he been preparing the preſent volume according to his original intention for a wider circle of readers he ſhould have deemed the addition of a large body of explanatory notes abſolutely indiſpenſable.

Owing, however, to the reprint having been undertaken by the Roxburghe Club, he has confined his remarks within as narrow limits as poſſible.

The ſhields of the Counteſſes of Hertford and Nottingham, and that of Lord Chancellor Hatton, are placed before the titles of the poems dedicated to their reſpective memories; but the perſon intended under the name of "Emaricdulfe" being unknown, that work is neceſſarily deprived of a ſimilar embelliſhment.

The tract on Lord Chancellor Hatton, it will be obſerved, is, with the exception of the title-page, not executed in facſimile like the others; a difference which was cauſed by the adoption of facſimile reproduction having been determined on after that tract had been already printed.

The ſhields and title-page were engraved by Mr. J. A. Burt; by whom alſo the latter was deſigned.

CHARLES EDMONDS.

2

HONI·SOIT·QVI·MAL·Y·PENSE

·AMO·

A
LAMPORT
GARLAND

COMPRISING

EMARICDULFE
By E. C. Esquier.
London, 1595.

CELESTIALL ELEGIES
By Thomas Rogers Esquire.
London, 1598.

VERTUES DUE
By T. P. Gentleman.
London, 1603.

A COMMEMORATION
on Sir Christopher Hatton.
By John Phillips.
London, 1591.

PRINTED FOR THE
ROXBURGHE CLUB.
MDCCCLXXXI.

EMARICDULFE.

EMARICDULFE.

THE prefent collection of Sonnets is printed from an unique and hitherto unknown work, which is bound up with three other Poetical Tracts of great rarity and value, namely, Barnfielde's Cynthia, 1595; Griffin's Fidefsa, 1596; and Tofte's Laura, 1597.

Its claims to the honour of a reprint are not merely on account of its rarity. In fome parts the Sonnets fhow great excellence, both in thought and expreffion; but in mufical rhythm they are perhaps—with fome exceptions where the lines, though they each scan, read more like profe than poetry—of better quality than they are in fonnet-fenfe. One peculiarity is, as compared with Shakespeare's poetry of the fame date, the frequent ufe of an extra syllable, as is apparent in Sonnet VII. This is noticeable, becaufe it fhows that the ufe of this extra fyllable, and Shake-fpeare's increased ufe of it as his years went on, was not even a femi-originality.

Another fource of intereft is the obfcurity which involves both the writer and the object of his adoration, for the whole work is devoted to the expreffion of love for a lady who is concealed under the remarkable pfeudonym of *Emaricdulfe*, by her admirer, who is equally succeffful in concealing himself under the initials *E.C.* Yet this obfcurity arifes perhaps only from lapfe of time, for when a difcarded lover commits his forrows to the prefs, and this with the tacit confent of the lady—when initials (no doubt true ones) and a pfeudonym (perhaps in deference to the fame) are affixed to the title-page—and when friends with well-known names are appealed to—it is hardly conceivable that the names of the lovers and the circumſtances of their connexion could long eſcape the knowledge of their contemporaries; eſpecially as both belonged—as is demonſtrable from the tone of the dedication and the names mentioned therein—to the upper claſſes of ſociety.

Much reſearch has been made by the Editor and others to ſolve the myſtery of theſe ſaid initials of ' *E. C.*' and of the evidently compoſite name of *Emaricdulfe*—or, as it is ofteneſt ſpelt, *Emaricdulf*—but without ſucceſs. As to the initials; it is to be obſerved that a writer uſing the ſame has verſes "In prayſe of Gaſcoignes Poſies," before the latter's poems; but it muſt be confeſſed that they more probably belong to an older man than the E. C. now in queſtion. Yet it is quite poſſible that other explorers into literary myſteries may be more fortunate, and that the identity of the parties may at a future time be eſtabliſhed when leaſt expected. With this object in view, therefore, the Editor ventures to print, *in extenſo*, the following verſes (on the reverſe of the leaf containing which are the names of the ſpeakers in the play), which are ſubſcribed with the ſame initials 'E. C.', as it is not abſolutely impoſſible that they emanated from the author of our tract. They were previouſly communicated to *Notes and Queries*, Ser. III. vol. 8. (9 Sept. 1865) by Mr. W. Carew Hazlitt, who introduces them thus:—

"In examining ſome old books and MSS. for a different purpoſe, I came acroſs a copy of 'The Tragedy of Mariam, the Fair Queen of Jewry,' 1613, by Lady E. Carew, with a Dedication, which I never met with before in copies of this drama, as follows :—

TO DIANAES

EARTHLIE DEPVTESSE,

and my worthy Sister, Mistris

ELIZABETH CARYE.

———

When cheerfull *Phœbus* his full courſe hath run,
His ſiſters fainter beams our harts doth cheere:
So your faire Brother is to mee the Sunne,
And you his Siſter as my Moone appeere.

You are my next belou'd, my fecond Friend,
For when my *Phœbus* abfence makes it Night,
Whilft to th' *Antipodes* his beames do bend,
From you, my *Phœbe*, ſhines my fecond Light.

Hee like to *SOL*, cleare-ſighted, conſtant, free,
You, *LUNA*-like, vnfpotted, chaſt, diuine:
Hee ſhone on *Sicily*, you deſtin'd bee,
T'illumine the now obfcurde *Paleſtine.*
My firſt was confecrated to *Apollo,*
My fecond to *DIANA* now ſhall follow.

E. C.

The alluſions in the above verſes to "hee ſhone on Sicily" may be either to ſome Works or ſome Travels of her brother, in the ſame ſenſe as the reference to the "now obfcurde Paleſtine" indicates her own tragedy of "Mariam." In the Catalogue of the Harleian MSS. in the Britiſh Muſeum (No. 6917) is mention of "Sir George Carew's Poems"; but this is an error, for they prove to be not by him but tranfcripts of thoſe by Thomas Carew. There being ſeveral families bearing the names Carew and Carey (which were uſed indifcriminately by all of them), it is not impoſſible that the Beddington Carews may have furnifhed the authoreſs of "Mariam." Sir Francis Carew fucceeded his father Sir Nicholas in 1539, and died in extreme old age (81) in May 1611, having had no iſſue. (See Nichols's Progreſſes of James I. vol. 1. p. 164). His heir was his ſiſter's ſon, Sir Nicholas Throckmorton, who then aſſumed the furname of *Carew*. This Sir Nicholas (who was brother-in-law to Sir Walter Ralegh) had a daughter, *Elizabeth*, who might have been the authoreſs of "Mariam"; and ſhe had likewiſe *brothers*, namely Francis (who died in 1649, and whoſe ſon, Sir Nicholas, married Suſan, daughter to Sir Juſtinian Iſham, Bart.), Nicholas, George, and *Edmund*. This latter may have been the writer of the "Dedication."

After this digreſſion, we will return to the Sonnets—which, according to the author's Dedication, were "begun, at the command and ſervice

of a faire Dame," and which refer to one fubject—the glorification of his
lady-love.   That his addreffes were at one time favourably received may
be gathered from feveral of the Sonnets, and that the couple ftood on
intimate terms towards each other may be inferred from Sonnet VII.,
in which he is compelled to exprefs contrition for his overbold prefumption
on one occafion by which he incurred her difpleafure.   That he had,
moreover, fome grounds for anticipating a favourable iffue for his fuit
is hinted at in Sonnet XIII., in which he expatiates on their mutual
love, of which her prefents to him were an evidence.   And this ftate of
things is reiterated in Sonnet XXVII.   But afterwards he feems to have
abandoned all hope of obtaining her, and the remaining Sonnets fhow that
he was certain of ultimate rejection.   Yet, notwithftanding this downfall
of his hopes, it is fufficiently clear from paffages in the later Sonnets,
and in the Dedication—which was naturally the laft portion written—
that the couple retained kindly feelings for each other; ftrengthened
perhaps by the fact that her choice of a hufband was not a happy one.
But, be the latter conjecture true or not, it is certain that the Dedication
points to fome domeftic embroilment or fcandal which has advifedly been
left unintelligible except to the parties concerned.

At the clofe of the laft Sonnet are clear allufions to the poets Daniel
and Spenfer, and to Queen Elizabeth.   Thefe, however, throw no light
on the date of the compofition of the body of Sonnets, which were publifhed in 1595.   The former's collection of Sonnets, entitled "Delia," firft
appeared in print in 1592 ; and the firft part of Spenfer's "Faerie
Queene," which is no doubt the work alluded to, in 1590.

As to the choice of the name "Emaricdulf" (more rarely "Emaricdulfe") ; it is doubtlefs a pfeudonym, like the "Laura" of Tofte, the
"Fideffa" of Griffin, the "Cynthia" of Barnfielde, the "Delia" of Daniel,
etc.   Unlike them, however, it is a pfeudonym compofed, in all pro-
bability, of the letters of the real name of the lady commemorated.   But
it feems impoffible to difcover in the Sonnets any clue to this name.
They are full to overflowing of praife of her "more than heavenly
parts" ; her wifdom, chaftity, beauty, fkill in mufic, etc. but filent with

reference to her lineage or any other circumftance from which bio-graphical or genealogical facts might be inferred.

That the author intended the word to be pronounced "E-marric-dulf" is clear from the rhythm, and from his fpelling it, throughout the fixteen fonnets in which it forms part of the verfe (with a fingle exception in Sonnet IV), without the final *e*. On the title-page, and in the firft heading alfo, it has this final vowel. Why this variation fhould have been made it is difficult to fee, unlefs it were the whim of the printer. "Emaric" occurs in Sonnet XII.; but this name applies to another perfon than "Emaricdulf"—in fact to "a young Emaricdulf"—a boy, who is fpoken of alfo in Sonnet XI.

Edward Fitton—one of the gentlemen to whom the work is dedicated —was probably the fon of Sir John Fitton, of Gawfworth, Chefhire, and the one who fubfequently (2 Oct. 1617) was created a Baronet. The other friend—John Zouch—was apparently one of the Zouches of Haryngworth. Full particulars of thefe families will be found in Betham's Baronetage of England. 5 Vols. 4to. 1801-5.

A.j.

Emaricdulfe.

SONNETS
WRITTEN BY
*E.C.*Esquier.

Non sunt vt quondam, plena fauoris erant.

AT LONDON,
Printed for *Matthew Law.*
1595.

TO MY VERY GOOD
friends, *Iohn Zouch,* and *Ed-*
ward Fitton, Esquiers.

BOth louing friends, forasmuch as by
reason of an ague, I was inforced to
keepe my chamber, and to abandon
idlenes, I tooke in hande my pen to fi-
nish an idle worke I had begun, at the command
and seruice of a faire Dame, being most exqui-
sitly well featured, and of as excellent good car-
riage, adorned with vertue: and vnderstanding
the storie, and knowing you both to be of sufficient valour, wit, and honestie, presumed to dedicate the same to you, not doubting but that you
will vouchsafe for my sake, to maintaine the honour of so sweete a Saint. Thus crauing you my
deare friends to be patrones of these fewe Sonnets: being well perswaded you will excuse my

A 3   *vnlearned*

The Epistle.

nlearned writing, in regard you may be assured
I am no scholler, as dooth appeare by this my
worthles verse: hoping you will receive my good-
will with content, as I my selfe shall be then best
satisfied. And so wishing you both as much
comfortable happines, as to my soule:
I bid you heartily farewell.

Yours in all true friend-
ship. E.C.

EMARICDVLFE.

SONNET. I.

WHen first the rage of loue assail'd my hart,
  And towards my thoughts his fiery forces bent:
Eftsoones to shield me from his wounding dart,
  Arm'd with disdaine, I held him in contempt.
Curld headed loue when from mount Erecine
  He saw this geere, so ill thereof he brookes,
That thence he speedes vnwilling to be seene,
  Till he had tane his stand in thy faire lookes.
There all inrag'd his golden bow he bent,
  And nockt his arrow like a pretie elfe:
Which when I saw, I humbly to him went,
  And cri'd hold, hold, and I will yeeld my selfe.
Thus *Cupid* conquer'd me, and made me sweare
Homage to him, and dutie to my deare.

A 4   Homage

SONNET. II.

HOmage to loue, dutie to thee my deare,
  Deare mistris of my thoughts, Queene of my ioyt
Then my lifes gratious planet bright appeare,
  My hearts deepe griefe and sorrow to destroy,
Be not (I thee beseech) my cares maintainer:
  For in thy power it lyes to saue or strike,
To kill the griefe, or els the griefes retainer,
  With loue or hate the infant of dislike.
O if that cruell loue did not command
  To slay my heart without remorse or pitie:
Or if he did that sad doome countermand,
  And be a gratious Queene of gentle mercie:
Sweet shew thy selfe diuine in being pitifull,
For nature of the gods is to be mercifull.

Why

SONNET. III.

WHy doe I pleade for mercie vnto thee,
  When from offence my life & foule are cleere?
For in my heart I neere offended thee,
  Vnleffe the hie pitch of his flight it were.
I, that is it, I to too well confider,
  Thy fparkling beautie is the funne that melted:
My thoughts the waxe that ioyn'd his wings together,
  And till my very fall I neuer felt it:
Defpaire the Ocean is that fwallowed me,
  Where I like Icarus continue drowned,
Till with thy beautie I reuiued be,
  And with loues immortalitie be crowned.
True loue immortall is, then loue me truly:
Sweet doe, and then thy name Ile honor duly.

                                    My

SONNET. IIII.

MY forlorne muse that neuer trode the path
  That leades to top of hie Pierion mount,
Nor neuer washt within the liuesome bath
  Of learnings spring, bright Aganippe fount:
Mine artles pen that neuer yet was dipt
  In sacred nectar of sweet Castalie,
My louesicke heart that euer hath I clipt,
  Emaricdulfe the Queene of chastitie:
Shall now learne skill my Ladies fame to raise,
  Shall now take paines her vertues to record,
And honor her with more immortall praise,
  Then euer heretofore they could affoord:
Both heart, and pen, and muse shall thinke it dutie,
With sigheswolne words to blaze her heauenly beutie.
                                          Nature

SONNET. V.

NAture (*Emaricdulf*) did greatly fauour,
　　When firſt her pourtrait ſhe began to pencill,
And rob'd the heauens of her chiefeſt honour:
　　There ſacred beautie all her parts doth tincill.
Heauens Hyrarkie is in her bright eyes ſpheered:
　　The Graces ſport in her cheekes dimpled pits:
Trophies of maieſtie in her face be reared,
　　And in her lookes ſtately Saturnia ſits.
Modeſt Diana in her thoughts doth glorie,
　　Loue-lacking Veſta in her heart inthroned:
The quired Muſes on her lips doe ſtorie
　　Their heauen ſweet notes, as if that place they ow-
But aye is me, *Cupid* and *Venus* faire　　　　(ned.
Haue no degree, ſaue in her golden haire.

Within

SONNET. VI.

Wlthin her haire *Venus* and *Cupid* fport them:
 Sometime they twiſt it Amberlike in gold,
To which the whiſtling windes doe oft refort them,
 As if they ſtroue to haue the knots vnrold:
Sometime they let their golden treſſes dangle,
 And therewith nets and amorous gins they make,
Wherewith the hearts of louers to intangle
 Which once inthral'd,no ranſome they will take.
But as to tyrants ſitting in their thrones,
 Looke on their ſlaues with tyrannizing eyes:
So they no whit regarding louers mones,
 Doome worlds of hearts to endles ſlaueries,
Vnleſſe they ſubieᶜt-like ſweare to adore,
And ſerue *Emaricdulf* for euermore.

I

SONNET. VII.

I Will perseuer euer for to loue thee,
  O cease diuinest sweetnes to disdaine mee:
Albeit my loues true types can neuer moue thee,
  Yet from affection let not pride detaine thee.
Although my heart once purchast thy displeasure
  With ouerbold presumption on thy fauour:
Yet now Ile sacrifice my richest treasure
  Vnto thy name and much admired honour:
Teares are the treasure of my griefe-gal'd hart,
  Which on (thy loue) my altar I haue dropped
To thee, that my thoughts temples goddesse art,
  Hoping thy anger would thereby be stopped.
If these to get thy grace may not suffice,
My heart is slaine, accept that sacrifice:

                             Emo.

SONNET. VIII.

E *Mariedulf*, thou grace to euery grace,
   Thou perfect life of my vnperfect liuing:
My thoughts sole heaue, my harts sweet resting place.
   Cause of my woe and comfort of my grieuing.
O giue me leaue and I will tell thee how
   The haples place and the vnhappie time,
Wherein and when my selfe I did auow
   To honour thee, and giue my heart to thine.
Wearie with labour, labour that did like me,
   I gaue my bodie to a sweet repose :
A golden slumber suddenly did strike me,
   That in deaths cabbin euery sense did close :
And either in a heauenly trance or vision,
I then beheld this pleasing apparition.

A

SONNET. IX.

A Wight was clad most Foster-like in greene,
  With loyal horne and hunting pole in hand:
Whose chanting hoūds were heard in woods & seene
  The deere amasde before the rider stand:
The keeper bids goe choose the best in heard:
  The huntsman sayd, my chouse is not to change:
And drawing neere the deere was sore affeard,
  Into the woods the rider spurd to range:
There did he view a faire young barren doe
  Within the hey fast by the purley side,
And woodman-like did take the winde then soe,
  Whereby the deere might better him abide.
At length he shot, and hit the very same
Where he best likte and lou'd of all the game.

                                        But

SONNET. X.

BVt stay conceit where he best likt to loue,
  Yea better he if better best might bee:
The Rider thought the best of better proue,
  Till fortune sign'd his fortune for to see.
Now wearie he betooke himselfe to rest,
  Deuised where he might good harbour finde:
Emaricdulf (quoth he) I am her guest,
  And thither went: she greeted him most kinde:
Welcome sayd she, three welcomes more she gaue:
  His hand she tooke, and talking with him then,
What wine or beere to drinke wilt please you haue,
  Sixe welcomes more, and so she made them ten.
He dranke his fill, and fed to his desire,
Refresht himselfe, and then did home retire.

                                    Forth-

SONNET. XI.

FOrthwith I faw, and with the fight was bleft,
   A beautious iffue of a beautious mother,
A young *Emaricdulf*, whofe fight increaft
   Millions of ioyes each one exceeding other:
Faire fpringing branch fprong of a hopefull ftocke,
   On thee more beauties nature had beftowde,
Then in her heauenly ftorehoufe fhe doth locke,
   Or may be fcene difperft on earth abrode.
Thrife had the Sunne the world encompaffed,
   Before this bloffome with deaths winter nipt:
O cruell death that thus haft withered
   So faire a branch before it halfe was ripte !
Halfe glad with ioyes, and halfe appal'd with feares,
I wak't, and found my cheekes bedew'd with teares.

                    B   My

SONNET. XII.

MY cheeks bedew'd, my eies euē drown'd with teares
   O fearfull storme that caufde fo great a fhowre
Griefe ty'd my tongue, forrow did ftop my eares,
   Becaufe earth loft her fweeteft paramoure.
O cruell heauens and regardleffe fates !
   If the worlds beautie had compaffion'd you,
You might by powre haue fhut deaths ebongates,
   And been remorfefull at her heauenly view.
O foolifh nature why didft thou create
   A thing fo faire, if fairenes be neglected?
But faireft things be fubiect vnto fate,
   And in the end are by the fates reiected.
Yong *Ematic* yet thou eroft the deftinie,
For thou furuiu'ft in fame, that nere fhall die.

SONNET. XIII.

THat I did loue and once was lou'd of thee,
　Witnesse the fauours that I haue receiued:
That golden ring, pledge of thy conſtancie :
　That bracelet, that my libertie bereaued:
Thoſe gloues, that once adorn'd thy lillie hands:
　That handkercher, whoſe maze in thral'd me ſo:
Thoſe thouſand gifts, that like a thouſand bands
　Bound both my heart and ſoule to weale and woe.
All which I weare, and wearing them ſigh forth
　You inſtancies of her true ſoyaltie :
I doe not keepe you for your ſoueraigne worth,
　But for her ſake that ſent you vnto me :
Tis ſhe, not you, that doth compell my eyes,
My lifes ſole light, my hearts ſole paradice.

SONNET. XIIII.

ONe day,ô ten times happie was that day,
   Emaricdulf was in her garden walking,
Where *Floras* imps ioy'd with her feete to play,
   And I to fee them thitherward ran ftalking,
Behind the hedge(not daring to be feene)
   I faw the fweet fent Rofes blufh for fhame,
The Violets ftain'd,and pale the Lillies beene:
   Whereat to fmile my Ladie had good game.
Sometimes fhe pleafde to fport vpon the graffe,
   That chang'd his hew to fee her heauenly prefence:
But when fhe was imasked,then (alas)
   They as my felfe wail'd for her beauties abfence:
They mourn'd for that their miftris went away,
And I for end of fuch a bleffed day.

                        What

SONNET. XV.

WHat meane our Merchants so with eger minds
    To plough the seas to finde rich iuels forth?
Sith in *Emaricdulf* a thousand kinds
    Are heap'd, exceeding wealthie Indias worth:
Then India doth her haire affoord more gold,
    And thousands siluer mines her forhead showes,
More Diamonds then th'Egyptian surges folde,
    Within her eyes rich treasurie nature stowes:
Her hony breath, but more then hony sweete,
    Exceeds the odours of Arabia:
Those preuous rankes continually that meete,
    Are pearles more worth then all America.
Her other parts (proud *Cupids* countermare)
Exceed the world for worth, the heauens for state.

      B 3   Looke

SONNET. XVI.

Looke when dame *Tellus* clad in *Floras* pride,
 Her summer vaile with faire imbroderie,
And fragrant hearbs sweet blossom'd hauing dide,
 And spred abrode her spangled tapistrie :
Then shalt thou see a thousand of her flowers
 (For their faire hew and life delighting sauours)
Gathered to deck and beautifie the bowers
 Of Ladies faire, grac'd with their louers fauours.
But when rough winter nips them with his rage,
 They are disdain'd and not at all respected :
Then loue (*Ismariedulf*) in thy yong age,
 Lest being old, like flowers thou be reiected :
Nature made nothing that doth euer flourish,
And euen as beautie fades, so loue doth perish.

I

SONNET. XVII.

I Am inchanted with thy snow-white hands,
   That mase me with their quaint dexteritie,
And with their touch, tye in a thousand bands
   My veelding heart euer to honour thee:
Thought of thy daintie fingers long and small,
   For pretie action that exceed compare,
Sufficient is to blesse me, and withall
   To free my chained thoughts from sorrowes snare.
But that which crownes my soule with heauenly blis,
   And giues my heart fruition of all ioyes,
Their daintie concord and sweet musick is,
   That poysons griefe and cureth all annoyes,
Those eyes that see, those eares are blest that heare
These heauenly gifts of nature in my deare.

       Emi-

SONNET. XVIII.

E*Mariedulf*, if thou this riddle reade,
    This darke *Ænigma* that I will demand thee,
Then for thy wiſedomes well deſeruing meede,
    In loues pure dutie thou ſhalt ay command mee.
A Turtle that had choſe his louing mate,
    Sate ſeemly percht vpon a red roſe breere:
Yet ſaw a bird (ayres paragon for ſtate)
    That farre ſurpaſt his late eſpouſed deere:
He chang'd himſelfe into that luſtfull bird
    That *Iuno* loues, and to his loue reſorted:
And thought with amorous ſpeeches to haue ſirde
    Her conſtant heart: but her in vaine he courted.
When bootles he had woo'd her to his paine,
He tooke his leaue and turn'd his ſhape againe.

The

SONNET. XIX.

THe Heauens and Nature whē my Loue was borne,
  Stroue which of both fhuld moft adorne & grace
The facred heauens in wealthie natures fcorne (her:
  With wifedomes pure infufion did ēbrace her:
Nature lent wings to wifedome for her flight,
  And deckt my Ladie with fuch heauenly features,
As nere before appear'd in humane fight,
  Ne euer fcheuce in terreftriall creatures.
(Quoth Wifedome)I will guide her conftant hart
  At all affaies with policie to relioue her:
(Quoth Nature)I will caft thofe gifts apart,
  With outward graces that I meane to giue her.
Yet were they reconcil'd, and fwore withall
To make her more then halfe celeftiall.

                                        That

SONNET. XX.

THat thou art faire exceeding all compare,
   Witnes thy eyes that gaze vpon thy beautie,
Witnes the hearts thou daily dost insnare,
   And draw to honour thee with louers dutie:
That thou art wise witnes the worlds report,
   Witnes the thoughts that do so much admire thee,
Witnes the heauen-borne Muses that resort,
   And for their mistris meekly do desire thee :
That thou art both exceeding faire and wise,
   Witnes the anguish of my sillie hart:
Thy heauenly shape hath caught me by my eyes,
   Thy secret wisedome that giues art to art,
So circumuents me and procures my paine,
That I must dye, vnles thou true remaine.

All

SONNET. XXI.

AL those that write of heauen and heauenly ioyes,
　Defcribe the way with narrow crooked bedings,
Befet with griefe, paine, horror and annoyes,
　That till all end haue neuer perfect endings.
The heauen wherein my thoughts are refident,
　The paradice wherein my heart is fainted,
Through ftreet-like ftraight hie-waies I did attempt,
　Nor with rough care nor rigorous croffe attained.
I muft confeffe faith was the only meane,
　For that with fome for want thereof did miffe,
Only thereby at length I did obtaine,
　And by that faith am now inftal'd in bliffe:
There fleepe my thoughts, my heart there fet thy reft,
Both heart & thoughts thinke that her heauen is beft.
　　　　　　　　　　　　　　Ye

SONNET. XXII.

YE subiects of her partiall painted praise,
    Pen, paper, inke, you feeble instruments:
Vnto a higher straine I now must raise
    Your mistris beautious faire abiliments.
Thou author of our hie Meonian verse,
    That checks the proud Castalians eloquence:
With humble spirit if I now reherse
    Her seuerall graces natures excellence:
Smile on these rough-hewd lines, these ragged words
    That neuer stil'd from the Castalian spring:
Nor that one true Apologie affoords,
    Nor neuer learn'd with pleasant tune to sing:
So shall they liue, and liuing still perseuer
To deifie her sacred name for euer.

                    Ye

SONNET. XXIII.

YE moderne Laureats of this later age,
    That liue the worlds admirement for your writ,
And seeme infused with a diuine rage,
    To shew the heauenly quintessence of wit :
You on whose welrun'd verse sits princely beautie,
    Deckt and adorn'd with heauens eternitie,
See I presume to cote (and all is duetie)
    Her graces with my learnings scarsitie.
But if my pen (*Marcias* harsh-writing quill)
    Could feede the feeling of my thoughts desire,
And shew my wit coequall with my will,
    Then with you men diuine I would conspire,
In learned poems and sweet poesie,
To send to heauen my Ladies dignitie.

                                                    Oft

SONNET. XXIIII.

OFt haue I heard hony-tong'd Ladies speake,
  Striuing their amorous courtiers to inchant,
And from their nectar lips such sweet words breake,
  As neither art nor heauenly skill did want.
But when *Emaricdulf* gins to discourse,
  Her words are more then wel-tun'd harmonie,
And euery sentence of a greater force
  Then Mermaids song, or Syrens sorceries.
And if to heare her speake, *Laertes* heire
  The wise *Vlisses* liu'd vs now among,
From her sweet words he could not stop his eare,
  As from the Syrens and the Mermaids song:
And had she in the Syrens place but stood,
Her heauenly voyce had drown'd him in the flood.

                                   Let

SONNET. XXV.

LEt gorgeous *Tytan* blush for of her haire
    Each trannel checks his brightest summers shine
The cleerest Comets drop within the aire
    To see them dim'd with those her glorious eine:
Iuno for state she matchles doth disgrace,
    Surpassing eke for stature *Dyan* tall,
Venus for faire faire *Venus* for her face,
    In whose swert lookes are heap't the graces all:
For wisedome may she make comparison
    With *Pallas*, yet I wrong her ouer-much:
For who so sounds her policies each one,
    Will sweare *Trytonius* wit was neuer such:
Her she exceeds, though she exceed all other,
Being *Ioues* great daughter borne without a mother.

SONNET. XXVI.

E *Maricdulf* reade here, but reading marke
   As in a mirror my true conſtancie:
The golden Sunne ſhall firſt be turn'd to darke,
   And darkenes claime the Sunnes bright dignitie :
The ſtarres that ſpangle heauen with gliſtring light,
   In number more then ten times numberleſſe,
Shall ſooner leaue to beautifie the night,
   And thereby make the world ſeeme comfortleſſe
Firſt ſhall the Sea become the continent,
   And red-gild Dolphins dance vpon the ſhore :
Firſt wearie *Atlas* from his paine exempt,
   Shall leaue the heauens to tremble euermore,
Before I change my thoughts and leaue to loue thee,
And plead with words and direfull ſighs to moue thee.
                    Sweet

SONNET. XXVII.

SWeet are the thoughts of pleasures we haue vſde,
   Sweete are the thoughts that thinke of that ſame
Whoſe ſweetnes is too ſweet to be refuſde,   (ſweet,
   That vertuous loue-taſt for my faith was meet:
The taſte whereof is ſweeter vnto me,
   Then ſweeteſt ſweet that euer nature made.
No odours ſweetnes may compared be
   To this true ſweetnes that will neuer fade.
This Sonnet ſweet with cheerefull voyces ſing,
   . And tune the ſame ſo pleaſing to mine eare,
That *Emaricdulf* thy praiſes ſo may ring,
   As all the world thy honors fame may heare.
Once didſt thou vow, that vow to me obſerue,
Whoſe faith and truth from thee ſhall neuer ſwerue.

C   If

SONNET. XXVIII.

IF euer tongue with heauen inticing cries,
  If euer words blowne from a rented harr,
If euer teares shed from a Louers eyes,
  If euer sighes issue of griefe and smart,
If euer trembling pen with more then skill,
  If euer paper, witnes of true loue,
If euer inke, cheefe harbenger of will,
  If euer sentence made with art to moue,
If all of these combinde by *Cupids* power,
  My long borne liking to anatomise:
Had but the art, with art for to discouer
  What loue in me doth By his art comprise.
Then might the heauens, the earth, water and ayre,
Be witnes that I thinke thee onely fayre.

My

SONNET. XXIX.

MY hart is like a ship on *Neptunes* backe,
　Thy beautie is the sea where my ship sayleth,
Thy frownes the surges are that threat my wracke
　Thy smiles the windes that on my sailes soft gaileth
Long tost betwixt faire hope and foule despaire,
　My sea sick hart, arriued on thy shore:
Thy loue I meane, begges that he may repaire
　His broken vessell with thy bounteous store.
Dido relieu'd *Æneas* in distresse,
　And lent him loue, and gaue to him her heart
If halfe such bountie thou to me expresse,
　From thy faire shore I neuer will depart:
But thanke kinde fortune that my course did serte,
To suffer shipwrack on so sweete a porte.

On

SONNET. XXX.

ON *Tellus* bofome fpring two fragrant flowers,
  The milkwhite Lilly, and the blufhing Rofe,
Which daintie *Flora* for to decke her bowers
  Aboue all other colours chiefly chofe.
Thefe in my miftris cheekes both empire holding
  In emulation of each others hew,
Continually may be difcerned folding
  Beautie in lookes, and maieftie in view.
Sometime they meet, and in a skarlet field
  Warre with rebellious hearts neglecting dutie,
And neuer ceafe, vntill they force to yeeld
  Them coward captiues conquered by beautie.
Emaricdulf thus didft thou play the foe,
And I the rebell, and was conquer'd fo.

In

SONNET. XXXI.

IN tedious volumes I doe not intend
   To write my woes, my woes by loue procured,
Nor by my infant muse implore the end
   Of loues true life, this (loue) I haue abiured:
Only my face (faire deare) shall be the booke
   Wherein my daily care shall be rehearsed:
Whereby thou shalt perceiue when thou doest looke,
   How by thy beauties darts my heart was piersed.
My eyes shall witnes with distilling teares,
   And heart with deepe fetcht sighes shall manifest
My painfull torments causde by griefes and feares,
   And hourely labours mixt with deepe vnrest:
Both heart, and eyes, and face shall all expresse,
That only thou art cause of my distresse.

C 3

Thy

SONNET. XXXII.

THy image is plaine porturde in my thought,
    Thy conſtant minde is written in my heart,
Thy ſeemely grace and pleaſing ſpeech haue wrought
    To vow me thine, till death a ſunder part:
Thy fauours forſt me ſubiect vnto thee,
    Thy onely care extended to my good,
Ty louely lookes, commaunded all in me
    For thy deare ſake to ſpend my deareſt blood:
My ioy conſiſts in keeping of thy loue,
    My bale doth breede if I inioy it not :
My ſeruice true, from thee none can remoue,
    Vnleſſe both life and loue I ſhall forgot.
Though life and loue in time muſt haue an end,
Yet euer I haue vowde to be thy frend.

                                        Emp-

SONNET. XXXIII.

E *Maricdulf* my Orphan muses mother,
    Pure map of vertue, Honors onely daughter:
Bright gemme of bewtie, fayre aboue all other,
    True badge of faith, foule ignominies slaughter,
Ensigne of loue, soure enemie to lust,
    The graces grace, faire Eretines disgrace:
Wrongs cheefe reprouer, cause of what is iust,
    Aduices patron, councels resting place:
Wisdomes chiefe fort, wits onely pure refiner,
    Graue of deceite, the life of policie,
Fates best beloued, natures true diuiner,
    Nurce of inuention, hould of constancie,
Poyson of paine, Phisition of arroyes,
Elizivms pride, and paradice of ioyes.

C 4

Emarie-

S O N N E T. XXXIIIL.

E*Marted ull*, loue is a holy fire.
   That burnes vnseene, and yet not burning seene:
Free of himselfe, yet chain'd with strong desire :
   Conquerd by thee, yet triumphs in thy eine:
An eye-bewitching vision thee in seeming,
   That shadow-like flyes from a louers eyes :
An heauen aspiring spirit voyd of seeing :
   A gentle god, yet loues to tyrannize :
Bond-slaue to honour, burthen of conceit,
   The only god of thine eyes Hyrarkie,
Decay of friendship, grandsire of deceit,
   More then a god, yet wants a monarkie:
Bastard of nature, that to heauen did clime,
To seeme the misbegotten heire of time.

                            O

SONNET. XXXV.

O Faith, thou sacred Phœnix of this age,
, Into another world from hence exiled
Diuorc'd from honor by vnheedfull rage,
    Pure vertues nest by hatefull vice defiled:
Thou faith that cal'st thy firname Constancie,
    Christned aboue the nine-fold glorious sphere,
And from the heauens deriues thy pedegree,
    Planting the roote of thy faire linage there:
Let this thy glorie be aboue the rest,
    That banisht earth where thou didst once remaine,
Thou yet maist harbour in my mistris brest,
    So a pure chest pure treasure may containe,
And in her liuing beautie neuer old,
Seem like a pretious Diamond set in gold.

                                        When

SONNET. XXXVI.

WHen I behould heauens all behoulding ſtarres,
 I doe compare them to my woes and ſmart,
Cauſde by the many wounds and mightie ſcarres
 That loue hath trenched in my bleeding hart:
And when I thinke vpon the Ocean ſands,
 Me thinkes they number but my ladies bewties,
And repreſent the infinites of bandes
 Wherein my heart is bound to endles duties:
And when I ſee natures faire children thriue,
 Nurſt in the boſome of the fruitefull earth,
From my chaſt vowes they their increaſe deriue;
 And as they ſpring.ſo haue my vowes their birth:
And as the ſtarres and ſands haue endles date,
So is my loue ſubieſt to naught but fate.

         O

SONNET. XXXVII.

O Lust of sacred loue the soule corrupter,
  Vsurper of her heauenly dignitie,
Follies first childe, good councels interrupter
  Fostered by sloth, first step to infamie,
Thou hel-borne monster that affrights the wise,
  Loue-choking lust, vertues disdainefull foe :
Wisdomes contemner spurner of aduise,
  Swift to forsweare, to faithfull promise slow,
Be thou as far from her chast-thoughted breast,
  Her true loue kindled heart, her vertuous minde,
As is al-seeing *Tytan* from the west,
  When from *auroras* armes he doth vntwinde.
Nature did make her of a heauenly mould,
Onely true heauenly vertues to insould.

                               My

SONNET. XXXVIII.

MY thoughts afcending the hie houfe of fame,
  Found in records of vertuous monuments
A map of honours in a noble frame,
  Shining in fpight of deaths oft banifhments:
A thoufand colours Loue fate futed in,
  Guarded with honour and immortall time,
Luft led with enuie, feare, and deadly fin,
  Oppofde againft faire Loues out-fhining line.
True Conftancie kneeld at the feet of Loue,
  And begg'd for feruice, but could not procure it:
Which feene, my heart ftept forth & thought to moue
  Kind Loue for fauour, but did not allure it:
Yet when my heart fwore Conftancie was true,
I one welcom'd it, and gaue them both their due.

SONNET. XXXIX.

IMage of honour, Vertues first borne childe,
   Natures faire painted stage, Fames brightest face,
Syren that neuer with thy tongue beguild,
   Sibill more wise then Cumas Sibill was,
When learnings sun with more resplendent gleames,
   Shall with immortall flowres of poesie,
Bred by the vertue of Bram bigning beames
   Deck my inuention for thy dignitie:
With heauenly hymnes thy more thē heauenly parts
   Ile deifie, thy name commands such dutie,
Though many heads of poisest poets arts
   . Are insufficient to expresse thy beautie,
Thy name, thy honour, and loues puritie,
With Stanzas, Layes and Hymnes Ile stellifie.

Some

SONNET. XXXX.

SOme bewties make a god of flatterie,
 And scorne *Elizium*s eternall types,
Nathes,I abhorre such faithles prophesie,
 Least I be beaten with thy vertues stripes,
Wilt thou suruie another world to see?
 Delia sweete Prophet shall the praises singe
Of bewries worth exemplified in thee,
 And thy names honour in his sweete tunes ring:
Thy vertues *Collen* shall immortalize,
 Collen chast vertues organ sweeest esteem'd,
When for *Eliza* name he did comprise
 Such matter as inuentions wonder seem'd.
Thy vertues her,thy bewries shall the other;
Christen a new,whiles I sit by and wonder.

 Mea fortuna tua
 Vt hodie sit cras,& semper.
 FINIS. gd. E.C.

CELESTIALL ELEGIES.

ROGERS'S CELESTIALL ELEGIES.

THIS poetical Tract, like the others in the volume, is printed from an unique exemplar. Not only is no other copy known, but apparently no mention has been made of it by any Bibliographer or Biographer. It is marked by more ability and interest than the one which follows.

The author was poffibly the fame Thomas Rogers, a native of Gloucefterfhire (being born in or near to Tewkefbury), who lived moftly, in his latter days, in the parifh of St. Giles in the Fields, London, and who publifhed, in 1612, a funeral tribute to the memory of Prince Henry under the quaint (perhaps intended as a punning) title of "Gloucefters Myte." Dr. Blifs, who, in his edition of Wood's "Athenæ Oxonienfes," gives the concluding ftanza of it, mentions a copy as being in the Bodleian Library, but it is not known to exift elfewhere.

Some interefting allufions will be found fcattered through the work. Among them may be noticed the following:—In Quatorzain 8, Bajazeth and Tamberlaine. [Marlowe's play on this fubject was printed in 1590.] In Quatorzain 12, "Seas of troubles;" and "acting a part upon this worldly ftage". [The firft allufion here is curious, for Shakefpeare's play

of "Hamlet", in which it occurs, is fuppofed not to have been written before
1602-3]. In Quatorzain 13, a poor attempt at a pun. In Quatorzain
14, fome far-fetched Similes. In Quatorzain 14, allufions to " Thetis
ftreames", and " the rockes by Netleys fhores ", etc.

The " Ladie Fraunces, Counteffe of Hertford," here commemorated,
was the third daughter of Lord William Howard, firft Lord Howard of
Effingham (created Lord Admiral by Queen Mary), by his fecond wife,
Margaret, fecond daughter of Sir Thomas Gamage, and fifter of Charles,
fecond Lord Howard of Effingham, who was created Earl of Nottingham
in 1596. The latter was the chivalrous Lord High Admiral of England
who did fuch good fervice againft the Spanifh Armada in 1588, as well
as on other occafions. His firft wife was the Lady Katharine Cary,
daughter of Henry Cary, Lord Hunfdon, and the fubject of the following
poetical tribute by Thomas Powell: confequently the two ladies were
fifters-in-law.

The Countefs of Hertford died without iffue 14 May, 1598, aged
44, and was buried in the Chapel of St. Benedict, Weftminfter Abbey;
againft the eaft wall of which Chapel is a magnificent monument, twenty-
eight feet high, with a fuitable infcription to her memory.

" This monument occupies the place of the original altar, and was
probably erected within two years after the Counteff's demife, when the
two fteps to the altar were made to ferve as basements to it. This ftately
tomb is enriched with columns and pyramids of various kinds of marble,
decorated with the enfigns and devices of the noble families of Somerfet
and Effingham. The Countefs is reprefented in her robes, in a recum-
bent pofture, with her head refting on an embroidered cufhion, and her
feet on a lion's back." Abridged from *Ackermann's Hiftory of Weftminfter
Abbey*, vol. 2. p. 109.

Traces of the gold on the embroidery of the cufhion and of the
crimfon colour on the robes may ftill be observed.

This lady's eldeft fifter was named Douglas, and her career was an
extraordinary one. She was married, firft, to John Lord Sheffield;

fecondly to Robert Dudley, Earl of Leicefter; and thirdly, to Sir Edward
Stafford. An account of her intrigues with Leicefter (during her firft
hufband's life), will be found in Gervafe Holles's curious Memoirs of the
Holles family. Her marriage with Lord Leicefter, however, was denied
by him; and in confequence, her fon, the celebrated Sir Robert Dudley,
was declared illegitimate.

The principal events in the life of the Earl of Hertford are too
eafily acceffible to require a lengthened notice here. Suffice it to fay,
that, though the malice of the enemies of his father, the Protector
Somerfet, deprived him, after the fall of that great nobleman, of his
hereditary dignities and eftates, the favour of Queen Elizabeth, immediately on her acceffion, in November, 1558, reftored them to him.
But his firft marriage, very early in life, with Lady Catherine Grey (the
fifter of Lady Jane Grey), who had certain claims to the Succeffion,
provoked the ire of his fovereign to fuch an extent, that he was not
only fined by the Star Chamber in the fum of £15,000, but was, with
his unfortunate wife, committed to the Tower. After a captivity of four
years fhe was releafed, but never faw her hufband again. She died 26
January, 1567-8. The Earl was not releafed till he had fuffered nine
years' imprifonment. The fate of their grandfon, Sir William Seymour,
was fomewhat fimilar, for having married the Lady Arabella Stuart, her
nearnefs to the throne excited the jealoufy and apprehenfions of the
reigning fovereign, and led to her imprifonment, lunacy, and early death.

The Earl's fecond wife was the Lady Frances Howard—the fubject
of the following poetical tribute—who died in 1598, and by whom he
had no iffue.

His third wife, whom he married when he was upwards of fixty
years old, was alfo of noble defcent, and her character may be given in
the words of Granger (*Biographical Hiftory of England*). "She was
Frances, daughter to Thomas, Lord Howard of Bindon, fon to Thomas,
Duke of Norfolk. She was firft married to one Prannèl, a vintner's fon

in London, who was poffeffed of a good eftate. This match feems to
have been the effect of youthful paffion. Upon the deceafe of Prannel,
who lived but a fhort time after his marriage [he died in December, 1599],
fhe was courted by Sir George Rodney, a weft-country gentleman, to
whofe addreffes fhe feemed to liften ; but foon deferted him, and was
married to Edward, Earl of Hertford [about 27 May, 1601]. Upon
his marriage, Sir George wrote her a tender copy of verfes in his own
blood, and prefently after ran himfelf upon his fword. Her third hufband
was Lodowick, Duke of Richmond and Lenox, who left her [in February
1623-4], a very amiable widow. The aims of great beauties, like thofe
of conquerors, are boundlefs. Upon the death of the Duke, fhe afpired
to the King, but died in her ftate of widowhood [8th October, 1639, aged
63; leaving no children.] " " Her will, dated 28th July, and proved
31st October, 1639, is" (says Col. Chefter in his valuable 'Marriage,
Baptifmal, and Burial Regifters of Weftminfter Abbey 1875') "very long
and of marvellous hiftorical and genealogical intereft, and contains one
eccentric direction (for a lady of her years), viz: that her body fhall not be
opened, but packed in bran before it is cold, and buried wrapt in thofe
fheets wherein my lord and I firft flept that night when we were married."

She lies buried in Weftminfter Abbey, in the fame grave with her
third hufband—who, like herfelf and her fecond hufband, had been three
times married. The fplendid monument which covers their remains, and
which was erected by her, is thus defcribed in Ackermann's work on that
edifice.

" This tomb, which is of brafs, almoft fills the chapel to the north of
Henry the Seventh's monument. The figures of the Duke and Duchefs
are finely caft; but the caryatides, which fupport a canopy of various
ornamental pierced fcroll-work, in the characters of Faith, Hope, Charity,
and Prudence, poffefs fuperior excellence. The figure of Fame, on the
top, is reprefented in the act of taking her flight; and the urns are copied
after antique forms."

A curious account of this beautiful, attractive, and eccentric lady will be found in Arthur Wilson's Life and Reign of K. James I. published in 1653, folio. Lodge, however, in his "Portraits of Illustrious Personages of Great Britain," has inserted a less prejudiced life of the Duchess, to accompany her portrait, which is there engraved after a full-length picture by Vandyck, dated 1633, in the possession of the Marquis of Bath. Another engraved portrait of her by William Pas, dated 1623, after a painting by Van Somer, formerly possessed by Horace Walpole at Strawberry Hill, is prefixed to some presentation copies of Captain John Smith's History of Virginia, folio, 1624, a work dedicated to the Duchess.

A full length portrait of the Duke of Richmond, painted by Van Somer, dated 1623, aged 59, is in the possession of Her Majesty at Hampton Court.

The Earl of Hertford makes no figure in the politics of his time, but towards the end of the reign of Elizabeth he must have regained some portion of her favour, as we find that in September 1591 she visited him at his seat of Elvetham in Hampshire, where very elaborate entertainments, which occupied four days in representation and elicited her warm approval, were given in her honour. The account of these festivities is reprinted in Nichols's Progresses of Q. Elizabeth vol. iii. He was also one of the patrons of the Stage, for in 1592, according to the Privy Council Registers, he had among his servants a body of players ; who have, however, left few materials for the historian of the drama ; differing, in this respect, from the comedians under the protection of his brother-in-law, the Lord Admiral, who had connected with them in their management and concerns Philip Henslowe and Edward Alleyn. By James I. he was selected (in 1605) as one of the Ambassadors to the Archduke, an office which he accepted after much importunity, but which, in splendour at least, did not suffer at his hands, for Sir Dudley Carleton, writing to Mr. Winwood, says, "Our great Ambassadors draw near their time, and you may think all will be in the beſt manner, when the little Lord Hartford makes a rate of expence of £10,000, beſides the King's allowance."

The Earl of Hertford died in April 1621, at the advanced age of 83, and is buried with his unfortunate firſt wife in Saliſbury Cathedral, in the ſouth choir-aiſle, under a ſtately though taſteleſs monument. "It is worth while" (ſays Hallam, in his *Conſtitutional Hiſtory*, in which he diſcuſſes the claims of the Counteſs to the throne) "to read the epitaph on his monument; an affecting teſtimony to the purity and faithfulneſs of an attachment rendered ſtill more ſacred by misfortune and time. Quo deſiderio veteres revocavit amores."

Of Matthew Ewens, with whom the author of the preſent tract claims relationſhip, the following account is given in Foſs's *Judges of England*. "He was called upon to take the degree of ſerjeant by writ dated 29 November, 1593, the return of which was probably in the following Hilary term. During that term, on 1 February, 1594, he was raiſed to the bench of the Exchequer; and his judgments in that and the following years are reported by Savile and Coke. Beyond this no account appears of him; but his death or reſignation ſoon after occurred, as his ſucceſſor, John Savile, was appointed in July 1598."

CELESTIALL ELEGIES

of the Goddesses and the Muses, de-
deploring the death of the right honourable and vertuous
Ladie the Ladie FRAVNCES Countesse of Hertford,
late wife vnto the right honorable EDVVARD
SEYMOR Vicount Beanchamp
and Earle of Hertford.

WHEREVNTO ARE ANNEXED

some funerall verses touching the death of
MATHEVV EVVENS Esquire, late one
of the Barons of her Maiesties Court of Exchequer, vnto whome the author
hereof was allyed.

Propertius Eleg. 5. Lib. 3.
Haud vllas portabis opes Acherontis ad vndas
Nudus ad infernas stulte vehere rates.

Hor. Lib. 1. Ep. ad Quint
Mors vltima linea rerum est.

By *Thomas Rogers* Esquire.

Imprinted at London by *Richard Bradocke*, for
I. B. *and are to be sold at her shop in Paules*
Church-yard at the signe of the Bible.
1598.

To the Right

Honourable his singuler good Lord,
the Lord Edward Seymor viscount
Beauchampe Earle of Hertford.

 Ehold (*Right Honourable*) in
this *Theater of mortalitie a Tra-*
gedie, with a solemne funerall,
at which the Goddesses are chiefe mourners,
and the Muses attendants, wherein death
plaies the Tyrannicall King or the kinglie
Tyrant, your deare Ladie and wife the sub-
iect of his furie, which in a dumbe showe is
heere presented by me: whereof I desire your

A 2   Lord

Lordſhippe to be a Spectator and a Iudge
If I haue wittilie plaide the fooles part in
contriuing the matter (I thinke I haue plaid
the wiſeſt part :) And then I hope I ſhall.
haue your Lordſhips applauſe. And that is
all I expect.

Your Lordſhips euer at
commaund.

T. R.

Celestiall Eligies for the late death of
the right Honourable the Ladie Fraunces
Countesse of Hertforde.

QVATORZAIN. 1
Berecynthia.

(To wes,
DRawne in my Royall chariot, crownd with
   Through all the kingdoms of the centred earth
With a great Traine of the celestiall Powres
That from my wombe tooke their immortall birth,
Descend I as chiefe mourner from the skye,
To solemnize this Countesse funerall ,
And crowne her fame with immortalitie,
Although her bodie now to death be thrall
My daughter *Cynthia* whilome lou'd her deare,
Noble she was by vertue, birth, and match,
Match'd with a Peare, yet matchles without Peare,
For Pearelesse she, did others ouer match,
   Wherefore the Fates growne enuious of her praise
   For vertues sake, ab 'idg'd her earthlie daies,

A 3   I

QVATORZAIN. 2.

Iuno.

I that am both *Ioues* sister and his wife,
The Queene of heauen, whom Gods & men adore
Hearing the fame of this braue Ladies life,
In mournfull habit now her death deplores
She hath putt of all earthly ornaments
And cloth'd her soule in glories spotlesse robe,
She hath exchang'd these mixed Elements,
For that pure Quintessence, the heauenlie globe
Loe how her spright infranchised from thrall,
Of sinfull flesh, ascends the Christall skye,
Scorning to dwell long in this earthly vale,
Where all men rise to fall, and liue to die:

    Therefore she soard aboue a humane pitch,
    And with her vertues doth my Realme inrich.

                   Th

QVATORZAIN. 3.
Pallas.

THe pompe of this vaine world she did despise,
Weighing the slipperie state of earthly things,
Therefore aboue the Spheares of heauen she flies,
To sing and ioy before the King of Kings:
Her vertues that did militate on earth,
Against the flesh, the deuill, sinne and hell,
Now triumphe in the heauens, and conquer death
And in *Ioues* holy monarchie doe dwell.
I rue the losse of true Nobilitie
Whilome inuested in her noble breast,
Wisedome with honour link't in amitie,
VVere both in her, and she in death supprest:
How can *I* chuse but waile for her decease,
Sith by her death my kingdom doth decrease.

A 4   Ay

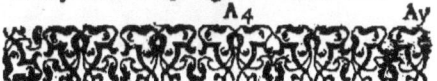

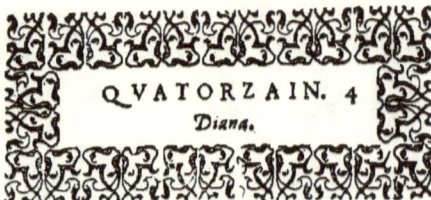

QVATORZAIN. 4
Diana.

AY me; my vestall flaine is now exrinct,
My flowre of *Chastitie* doth fade away
In *Lethes* flouds true noblenes doth sinke,
My Empyre runnes to ruinous decay;
Pittie, Almes-deeds and charitie is fled,
Fidelitie beyond the seas is gone,
True friendship now and faithfull loue is dead,
And *Priapus* vsurpeth *Cupids* throne :
She that did feeke my kingdome to maintaine,
By fanctitie, religion, faith, and zeale,
Through enuie of the Destenies is flaine,
Death robs th'Eschequer of my common weale,
  For all thofe rites which I was wont to haue,
  Are fled to heauen or buried in her graue.

If

QVATORZAIN. 51
Venus.

IF that I am a starre, Ile loose my light ,
And fall from Heauen, vpon the earth to morne,
Becaufe her lifes faire day is turndē to night,
My ioye to griefe, my loue to hate fhall turne.
If that I am a Goddeffe as menfay,
Whom louers tearme Celeftiall and deuine,
With humaine teares Ile wafh my ioyes away,
And on the earth no more by day-time fhine:
If I be beauties Soueraigne, and loues Queene,
Ile put a marke of clouds before my face,
Hating to loue , louing to liue vnfeene,
I will obfcure my felfe in fome darke place:
   And if I be a Planet, while I raigne,
   Ile frown on th'earth where my delight is flaine.
                                        From

QVATORZAIN. 6.
Thetis.

FRom th'vnknowne kingdome of th' Antipodes,
And from the fartheſt bonds of th' Ocean maine,
Attended with troopes of *Nereides*,
And charming *Syrens*, that ſupporte my traine:
Mou'd with the gentle murmure of the ſtreames,
That ſeeme mi humane miſeries to weepe,
I that doe kiſſe the Sunnes tranſplendent beames,
When he in *Neptunes* boſome falls a ſleepe;
Come to this famous land in waues of woe,
Like to a Queene in mourning weedes araide,
Crowned with cares, becauſe mans mortall foe,
The Tyrant death, his tragick part hath plaide;
   Sea more lamentes tnan all the worlde beſide,
 * His true loues loſſe that late in England dyde.

                                              My

QVATORZAIN. 7
Ceres.

MY wealth decaies for want of Somers heat,
Somers heat fades because the Sunne is fled,
The Sunne is fled, becaufe his griefe is great,
His griefe is great, becaufe his ioye is dead ,
Hisioye is dead, fince his deare ladie dyde,
And fince his lady dide he euer mournde,
He euer mournde, for loffe of Natures pride,
For Natures pride, is now to afhes turnde,
To afhes turnde that was a *Phœnix* rare,
A *Phœnix* rare, of whom no other bred,
No other bred , that breedes the more my care,
The more my care, fith all in her is dead:
   O Heaues, why do you bring this land fuch dearth,
   As for to take a *Phœnix* from the earth.

I

QVATORZAIN.8.

Fortuna.

I that do turne the rowling wheele of chaunce,
The blinde light *Goddesse* of vnconstancie,
That sometime did the Romaine Peers aduance,
To sway the worlds imperiall Monatchie:
I that doe kings enthrone, annoynt, and crowne,
And ofte depose them from the Royall seate,
I that on mightie *Baiazeth* did frowne,
And made the baseborne *Tamberlaine* so great:
Lament that death hath got the victorie,
While *I* am faine to flie away for feare,
For where death raines, there ends my soueraintie,
He casts downe *Trophees* which I did vpreare,
  This Ladie whome I raisde to high degree,
  Dyde not by chaunce but fatall destenie,

Red

QVATORZAIN. 9.
Nemesis.

RE d hote with rage whose heart with griefe doth
I come from *Ioue* sell *Atropos* to chide, (bleede,
That cut too soone this Countesse vitall threede,
Wherewith her soule and bodie were fast tide:
While wicked men long liue in Ioy and pleasure,
She liu'd long time in sicknesse and in paine,
Who still accounted vertue her chiefe treasure,
And losse of worldly wealth heauens richest gaine:
Wherefore she fled to heauen, from whence I came,
And with reuenge to scourge mens insolence,
And those same ruthlesse destenies to tame,
That by this Ladies death *Ioues* wrath incence,
    Who let the wicked long time liue in pride,
    While she that best deserued, soonest dide.

                                        Though

QVATORZAIN, 10.
Bellona.

THough I am fearefull Goddesse of dread warre,
    That hate to liue Idly at home in peace,
With humane cries allured I come from farre,
In streames of bloude to rue this dames decease,
This Lady was a *Howard* and did springe,
Out of the antient Duke of *Norfolkes* race,
Whose ofspring did subdue the *Scots* stout king,
And from the field rebellious foes did chase,
Her brother still restes loyal to the Crowne,
And Scepter which faire *Cynthia* now doth wield,
By Seas he hath obtain'd his high renowne,
The other by his conquest in the field,
    Wherefore I vow by land and Sea to raise,
    Eternall triumphes to the *Howards* praise.

                                    Crowned

QVATORZAIN. 11

Flora,

CRowned with wreathes of Odoriferous flowrs,
Whose sent perfumes the Empire of the *Ayre*,
Among the rest of the immortall powers,
Vnto the land of *Albion* I repaire.
Where I with garlands will her Toombe adorne,
And make death proud with ceremonious rites,
That for this Ladies sake I doe not scorne,(delights;
To decke her Graue, with th'earths faire flowers
For sith the world was sweetned by her breath,
That breath'd rare vertues forth, as then aliue,
Ile beautifie her Sepulcher, since death
Of her sweete sowle her body did depriue,
  For this braue dame was a sweet springing flower,
  Bedewde with heauenly grace till her last howre.
                                        From

QVATORZAIN, 12.
Proserpina.

FRom the black kingdome of infernall *Dis*,
All circumscrib'd with Characters of woe,
And from the dungen of the darke abysse,
Wherein the Ocean Seas of troubles flowe,
I doe ascend vpon this worldly stage,
In this sad Tragedie to act a part,
Sith she that was a light to that last age,
Is now confounded by deaths fatall darte;
The cruell destinies were much to blame,
To cut her threede of life ere throughly spunne,
Her life burnd out like to a *Tapers* flame,
And thus the howrglasse of my ioyes is runne :
    Wherefore the Fatall sisters shall repent
Her bodies death, and faire soules banishment.

I

QVATORZAIN. 13.
Aurora.

I now shall blush to kisse the Sunns faire face,
Or bid *bon Iour* vnto this hemyspheare,
I rather will lament in dolefull case,
The losse of her whom I did loue so deare,
I am the Muses euer constant friend
And sith she was their Matrone while she liu'd
I will bewaile for her vntimely ende,
By whom the sacred Sisters were releu'd:
I muse what Muse there is that will not weepe
When *I* shall tell this lamentable story,
That she is dead and now in dust doth sleepe,
Although her soule is crown'd with lasting glory.
  I thinke the world wilbe dissolu'd to teares,
  When this said tale shall penetrate mens eares.

B   Atty.

QVATORZAIN, 14.
Nox.

Attyrde in black spangled with flames of fier,
Imbroidered with starres in silent night ,
While *Phœbus* doth the lower world inspire,
with his bright beames & côsort breathing spright,
I come in clowds of griefe with pensiue soule,
Sending forth vapours of blacke discontent,
To fill the concaue Circle of the Pole,
And with my teares bedeawe each continent:
Because that she that made my night seeme daye,
By her pure vertues euer shining lamps,
Now makes my night more blacke by her decay,
Wandring with Ghosts in the *Elisian* Camps:
  Wherefore I still will weare a mourning vaile.
  For she is dead and humane flesh is fraile.

Ad ewe

QVATORZAIN. 15.
Gratia.

A Dewe faire *Venus* Ladie of delight,
Welcome pale horror griefe and discontent,
Come let vs wander to the vaile of night,
And for this Ladies death sighe and lament,
Our hopes late deade ingender liuing teares,
Our griefes awake doe bringe our ioyes asleepe,
Now we from *Thetis* streames will borow teares,
And teach the rockes by *Netleys* shores to weepe,
Our faire complexion is with sorrow chang'd,
We haue bin fellowe Mates with beauties Queene,
But from out selues we now are so estrang'd,
We are but shadowes of what we haue beene,
  And thus in vaine we daily doe deplore,
  For losse of life which we cannot restore,

QVATORZAIN, 17.
Horae.

WE that are calde Tymes goldē winged Howres:
   And are the Porters of Heauens Christall gate,
Comme from the Pallace of Celestiall powers,
This Countesse death with pompe to celebrate;
By shutting vp Heauens gate we send downe rayne,
Darking the triple region of the Aire,
And when we list opening the doore againe,
Dry the moyst clowdes & make the weather faire,
Weepe now O clowdes vppon the grassie earth,
With often drops sret through the hardest stones,
While we in sorrowe for this Ladies death,
Flie back againe to the Celestiall thrones:
   And locking fast the great Porte of the Skie,
   Send downe more showres for her mortalitie.

1

QVATORZAIN, 18.
Pandora.

I bring a box wherein all woes are closde,
Mingled with teares distild from sacred eyes,
And not so much as hope for me reposde
Is left behinde but quite away it flies·
The graces wherewith all the Gods indue me,
Are gone from me and to Ioues throne resort,
The blessings which vntill this day pursude me,
Forsake me now and I stand all amort.
Like *Niobe* that euer till death still mourn'de,
For her deare childrens losse whom *Phoebus* slue,
And to a senceless stone at last was turnde,
That in her life did most extreamely rue:
    And thus transformde I will become a Toombe.
    T'enclose her vertues in my dying woombe.

If

QVATORZAIN. 18.
Pales Dea pastorum.

IF kingdomes waile shall not the Cottage weepe?
   If the Court greeue shall not the Country grone?
If they doe morne that doe strong Lions keepe?
Shall not I, that keepe tender sheepe, bemoue?
If faire *Elisa* monarch of this Ile,
This Ladies losse doth gratiously lament,
It ill becomes a country swayne to smyle,
Or me that am the Shepheards presidente:
O thou rare *Queene* that makest the femal gender,
By much, more worthie then the Masculine,
To thee all praise and glorie I surrender,
Whom I esteeme as sacred and deuine;
   Had not thy life giuen shepheards sweet releefe,
   I should haue well nigh perished with greefo.

                                                  Euen

QVATORZAIN, 19.
Feronia.

EVen in this sad and melancholy moode,
With *Siluan Nimphes* which on me daily tende
Mated with sorrowe come I from the woode,
And to faire *Cynthias* kingdome now I wende,
Where the immortall Goddesses arriu'd,
At *Troynouant,* by which *Thames* waues do glide,
Where late a Ladie of great honour liu'd,
But greater vertue, that vntimely dyde:
Thither goe I among the rest to mourne,
And offer vp my teares vpon her shrine,
My loftie trees I will cut downe and burne,
In witnesse of her death for which I pyne:
  And as my trees consume away with flame
  So doth my heart with griefe, and ioy with shame.

B 4   In

QVATORZAIN. 15.
Libitina.

IN dreary accents of a doleſull verſe,
Ile ſpeake her praiſe though I haue longbin dūbe,
In ſable weedes ile decke her diſmall hearſe,
And ſacrifice my tears vppon her toombe:
With golden Statues ſhall her toombe be gilte,
Like King *Mauſolus* ſtately monument,
Which his deare wife the *Queene* of *Caria* built
To be the worldes eternall wonderment.
Or elſe I will her ſenceleſſe corps interre,
In ſome faire graue like the *Pyramides*,
And will enbalme her bodie with ſweete Mirrh
With *Caſſia*, *Ambergreece* and *Aloes*   (ſmell,
 That th'Ayre perfum'd therewith ſhall ſweetly
  While heauenly powers ſhal ring her woſull knel.

An-

 Erecinthia *alias Rhea Cybele Ops Ve-
sta, Tellus, &c.* as *Hesiodus* saith was
the daughter of *Coelum* and *Terra* the
wife of *Saturne*, commonly called the
mother of the gods & goddesses of the
earth; whome Poets faine to be drawne by foure
Lionsin a chariot with a crowne of Towres on her
head and a royall scepter in her hand, she is also re-
puted the founder of Cities and Towres for defence.

Iuno called *Prounba* and of some *Lucina* the
daughter of *Saturne* and *Ops*, wife and sister of *Iupiter*, Queene of heauen, and goddesse of riches, im-
palled with the celestiall diademe, drawne in her
chariot by Peacockes, she is accounted to predomi-
nate marriages, and the birth of children.

Pallas otherwise called *Minerua* as *Hesiodus* affirmeth is the daughter of *Neptune* and *Triton*, poetically

tically alſo fayned to be engendred of the braine of
Jupiter: She is the Goddeſſe of wiſedome, learning,
and the liberall ſciences, She is the ſiſter of *Mars*
and is ſaid to be the Goddeſſe of warres and martiall
ſtratagems, and for that is olten called *Bellona*.

Cynthia called alſo *Diana* and *Phœbe* the daughter
of *Iupiter* and *Latona* the ſiſter of *Phœbus* ſhe is the
Goddeſſe of hunting and fiſhing, who addicting her
ſelfe wholy to virginitie obtained of *Iupiter* therefore to liue in the woods. *Virgil. Lib. 11. Alme tibi hāc
nemorum cultrix Latonia virgo.*

Venus termed alſo *Cytherea* poetically ſained to
be bred of the froth of the Sea, excelled all other
Goddeſſes in beautie, ſhe is the Goddeſſe of loue,
pleaſures and laſciuious delightes, ſhe rideth in a chariot drawne by doues, ſhe is the mother of *Cupid* and
is accounted one of the ſeuen planets

Thetis

Thetis called alſo *Amphitrite* the wife of *Peleus* King of *Theſſalie*, daughter of *Nereus* and mother of *Achilles* was eſteemed Goddeſſe of the Sea: of *Nereus* all the Nymphes were called *Nereides*.

Ceres the daughter of *Saturne* and *Ops* ſiſter of *Iupiter* & *Pluto*, is the Goddeſſe of Corne drawen in her chariot by dragons, crownde with ſheaues of wheat ſhe wandred about the world to ſinde her daughter *Proſerpina* whom *Pluto* ſtole a way, ſhe firſt taught the vſe of the plough and to till the land.

Aurora the morning, the daughter of *Hyperion* and *Thia* in the iudgement of *Heſiodus*, or as others ſay of *Titan* and *Terra* whom for her fatre vermilion colour *Homer* faineth to haue fingers of damaske roſes, and to be drawne by bright bay horſes in a golden chariot, ſhe is ſaid by *Orpheus* not only to be a moſt comfortable Ladie to men, but alſo to beaſts and plants and is a great friend to the Muſes.

Nux

Nox the night, bred of *Chaos* as Poets faine whom they cal the most auntient mother of all creatures, because there was no light but darkenes before the Sunne and the heauens were made. And she possessed all places before the birth of the gods, she is cloathed in blacke rayment, with a sable vayle vpon her head, transported by blacke horses in her eben chariot, she came from *Erebus* and the infernals obscuring this Hemysphere when the Sunne is gone to the *Antipodes.*

Flora called also *Chloris* the wife of *Zephirus* is deemed the goddesse of Flowres:

Bellona the goddesse of warre called also *Pallas*, which to expresse both the valour and the wisedome of the honorable race of the *Howardes* I haue twise expressed in seuerall sonnets, whom *Virgil* nameth the president of warre.

Armi-

Armipotens bellæ præses Tritonia Pallas

Fortuna as some suppose was the daughter of *Oce-ānus*, albeit *Hesiodus* writing of the originall birth of the Gods, makes no mention of her, yet she is vainely reckoned among the number of the Gods as *Iuuenal* witnesseth.

> *Nullum numen abest si sit prudentia, sed te*
> *Nos facimus Fortuna deam Cœloᵹ̃ locamus.*

, She is the Goddesse of chance and inconstancie she is saide to be blinde and to be rouled about vp-on a wheale as *Tibullus* in 1. *Elegiarum. Versatur celeri Fors leuis orbe rota.*

Proserpina called also *Persephone* and of some *He-cate* is the daughter of *Iupiter* and *Ceres*, the wife of *Pluto* Queene of Hell, she hath soueraigne power of dead bodies.

Nemesis

Nemefis the daughter of *Oceanus* and *Nox* may be called the Goddeffe of reuenge, who was fent from *Iupiter* to fuppreffe the pride and infolence of fuch as are to much puft vp with arrogancie for the fruitio of worldly felicitie: and therfore *Ariftotle Li. de mundo*, affirmeth *Nemefis* to be the deuine power and iuftice of God to punifh malefactors for their haynous crimes, and to diftribute to euery one accord ding to his demerits.

Libitina is the Goddeffe of Funeralls.

The Graces called *Gratie* or *Charites* the Graces daughters of *Iupiter* and *Eurynome* whofe names are *Aglaia, Euphrofyne* and *Thalia*, they were beautifull and the companions of *Venus*.

Hore the howres, daughters of *Iupiter* and *Themis*, are by *Homer* and other Poets faide to keepe the gates of heauen, and by opening of them to make faire weather, and by fhutting them to make foule
weather

weather, they fauour learning and aſſociate *Venus* and the Graces: They are imagined to haue ſoft feet and to be moſt ſlow of all the Goddeſſes, and ſtill to worke ſome new matter, they moderate and deuide the ſucceſſion of times.

Pandora, a Ladie imbelliſhed with all fayre ornaments of bodie and minde on whome euery one of the Gods beſtowed a ſeuerall gift of grace, was ſent by *Ioue* to *Prometheus* with all euils incloſed, faſt in a box or litle cofer, which gift being refuſed by *Prometheus* was by her brought to *Epimetheus*, who opening the couer of the box, perceiuing all thoſe euils to flie out ſuddenly ſhut the ſame, reſeruing only hope in the bottome thereof repoſed which he kept faſt: which hope you muſt imagine now that *Pandora* hath loſt in the cariage by reaſon of this moſt noble Counteſſe death,

Niobe

Niobe the daughter of *Tantalus* waxing insolent beyond measure for the beautie and goodly proportion of her children, insomuch that she compared or rather preferred her selfe in opinion of glory before *Latona* and her sacred ofspring was therefore by the decree of the Gods metamorphosed into a stone, and so became her owne bodies sepulcher; and her children were slaine by *Phœbus* and *Diana* with arrowes as Poets fayne.

Pales is the Goddesse of Shepheards in honour of whose diety Shepheards did celebrate certain games called *Palilia*.

Feronia the Goddesse of woods or groues whose temple (as *Strabo* writeth) was famous in the Citie *Soraetes*, and she with great deuotion was there worshipped, of whome there is no mention made touching her birth or education, notwithstanding she is reckoned soueraigne of the woods as *Virgil* writeth.

Et viridi gaudens Feronia luco.   Great

QVATORZIAN. 1

Clio.

GReat princes actes I vse to royalize,
 And from the Stigian ftouds their fame to faue,
And in the Criftall mirror of the skies,
With wits faire Diamond I their praife ingraue,
By me *Alcmenas* fonne is made deuine,
And faire *Califto* turned to a Beare
Now in the Starrie firmament doth fhine,
And with her light adornes this Hemyfphere,
And I will raife to heauen this hoble dame,
Aboue the pureft Element of fire,
And lo in Starres charaƈterize hir fame,
That time fhall not her glories date expire,
  And yet my heart in pittie takes remorfe,
  For her deare foule and bodies late diuorfe.
            C   Knowing

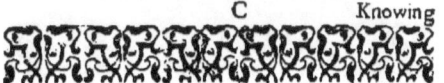

QVATORZIAN. 2

Melpomene.

KNowing her life what shall I sound her praise?
Or musing of her death fall in a sounde?
Shall I recorde her fame in my sweete laies?
Or by my sorrow make her death renownde?
I know not what to doe , I am amazde,
I wander in a Laborinth of woes,
Her praise alreadie through the world is blazd,
And now her death with greefe I must disclose;
Wherefore I register her death with teares,
Which doe turne blacke with sorrowe in the fall,
Wringing my handes renting my golden heares,
And with these reliques grace her funerall,
  Exclaming thus with euerlasting cries,
  Vertue grows sicke, shame liues, true honor dies.

I

QUATORZAIN. 3
Thalia.

I That in Princes Pallaces was bred,
　And did delight in euerie comicke sport,
Whose daintie feete on carpets vsde to treade,
And dance the measures statly in the court,
Will turne my mirthfull songs to dolefull cries,
And fill with teares the *Heliconian* brooke,
My louely cheekes besmeard withweeping eyes,
Like fleshlesse deathes Anatomie I looke,
For she that brought new reuels out of *France*,
When she returned to her natiue soyle,
Who sought my glory chiefly to aduance,
Hath now by death receiued a fatall foile,
　　Thus by hetlosse I am compeld to rue
　　That she to soone hath bid the world adewe.

　　　　　　Come

QVATORZAIN. 4
Euterpe.

COme sisters let vs sing sad roundelaies,
    And strew green Cypres boughs vpõ hir Tombe
Crowning her image with immortall bayes,
Oh sacred ofspring of *Latonas* wombe,
Play on thy seauen-strunge harpe and sadly warble,
The wa ifefull murmur of celestiall spheares,
And while thou doest engraue her fame in marble,
Ile digge her graue with showres of sacred teares;
My pipe shall make the stones to weepe for pitte,
As great *Amphions* Lyre did make them dance,
To build againe the ruynes of that Citie,
Which did maintaine the Grecian puisance,
    And yet not *Thebes* but *Troynouant* shall mourne
    For her whose flesh to Elements did turne.

                                                        What

QVATORZAIN. 5
Terpsichore.

VVHat dolefull *Diapason* shall I make,
　　What mournfull songs of sorrow shall I sing
What comfort in sweete Musicke can I take,
Sith death hath broke this Ladies vitall string:
My sacred Lyre that did resound of yore,
Celestiall harmony, like *Phœbus* Lute,
Such ioyfull accents now shall sound no more,
For inward sorrow makes our consort mute;
Sith death hath broke that string that did vnite
In mutuall loue her bodie and her soule,
My dulcimers shall make no more delight
And I will liue in euerlasting dole
　　For how can Musicke solace humaine eares,
　　Whē strings are broke & harts are drownd in tears

QVATORZAIN. 6.
Erato.

YE that like *Iulius Cæsar* seeke to measure,
  The spacious clymates of the centred round,
To fish for kingdomes and to purchase treasure,
Oppose your liues to euerie fatall wound :
Behold euen in the map of my sad face,
A true Cosmographie of humane woes,
For since foule death his Trophees heare did place,
In quiet rest I neuer could repose,
Vnto th'Antarticke Pole what need ye saile,
At home in safetie better may yee sleepe,
Consider by her death your flesh is fraile,
Sit downe by me vppon these rockes and weepe,
    Fot *Albion* now more sorrowes doth containe,
    Then there is wealth in all the Ocean mayne.
                                    Were

QVATORZAIN. 7
Calliope.

VVEre it not that *Eliza* did reuiue,
  My drooping spirits that are like to perish,
If that worlds myrrour onely she aliue,
Did not with bountie still my Poems cherish,
I should goe languish in some obscure caue,
Or with rude Satyres, & wood-nymphs should dwel
Learning should lie in base *Obliuions* graue,
And flow no more from *Aganippe* well:
But since this Ladies soule is vanished,
Out of this world (her corps to death enthrald)
She to a starre is metamorphosed
And with the golden Twinns in heauen enstald
      Or like the *Pleiades* enthron'd on high
      She may be term'd a *Phœnix* in the skie.

C 4   I saw

QVATORZAIN. 8.
Vrania.

I Sawe no fearefull comet in the Skye,
Nor firie Meteors lately did I viewe,
Whose dread aspect threatens mortalitie,
And losse of some great Princes to insue:
Nor by Astrologie did I deuine ,
That death so soone this Paragon should slay,
That she who did in grace and vertue shine,
Aboue her Peeres before them should decay,
I thinke while all the Gods in counsell sate,
To canonize some Saint, that late did die,
Not being mindfull of this Ladies state,
Whose fatall howre did then approach so nigh,
　　Death stole vppon her with his *Eben* darte
　　And vnwares did strike her to the heart.

　　　　　　　　　　　　　　　　　　Sith

QVATORZAIN.9.

Polyhymnia.

SIth I am tearm'd the Muses Oratrix,
My pen shall wright the Iliades of my greefe,
My tearefull eyes vppon her beare ile fixe,
My tongue shall tell a wofull tale in breefe:
My hands shall act the passions of my minde,
My ruthfull lookes bewray my pensiue thought,
I will complaine the Fates are too vnkinde,
Frō bad to worse the world still growes to nought:
Wherefore I thinke that *Plato's* wondrous yeare,
(When as the Orbs of Heauen shalbe reuolu'd,
To their first course) approcheth very neare
The bands ofth' Elements shalbe dissolu'd:
    And till those daies of consummation come,
    Cares make me passionate & sorrowes dombe.
                    Now

NOw *Goddesses* and *Muses* giue me leaue,
 In this sad Tragedie to acte a part,
I haue more cause for her decease to greeue,
Though you more wit to shew your sorrows smart:
Yee for affection doe extoll her praise,
And for mere pittie doe her death lament,
I both so. loue and duetie striue to raise
Her fame aboue the starrie firmament:
And death for enuie did abridge her daies
T'enrich his kingdome with this vertuous dame
But I for griefe that death the Tyrant plaies,
Impouerisht haue my wit t'enrich her fame
   While I performe these rites which are most fit,
   Death waxeth rich in spoyle, I spoild of witte.

                          An·

THE nine *Muſes* which are the preſidents of Poets and firſt authors of Poetry Muſicke & other
ſciences, are the daughters of *Iupiter* & *mnemoſyne*
alias memoria whoſe names are *Clio*, *Melpomine*,
Thalia, *Eutepre*, *Terpſichore*, *Erato*, *Calliope*, *Vrania* &
Polihimnia . *Clio* exerciſeth her wit & ſkill chiefely
in Hiſtories and recording the actes & monumēts
of worthie perſons, *Melpomine* in Tragedies, and
lamentable *Elegies*, *Thalia* in Comedies, comely
geſtures, and ſweete ſpeeches . *Euterpe* in the pipe
& ſuch like inſtruments, *Terpſichore* in the Citterne
or Lute, *Erato* in Geometrie, or Choſmographie,
Calliope in heroicke verſes, *Vrania* in Aſtrologie and
contemplation of the ſtarres, and *Polihimnia* in
Rhetoricke and Eloquence,

De-

Deuine sonnets dedicated to the said Lady not
long before her decease by the said Author.

Of Gods holy name, Iehouah, or Tetragrammaton.

THat name which *Moses* on his forehead bare,
  I in my heart doe worship and adore,
That name which Iewes to name did seldome dare,
May *I* presume for mercie to implore?
That name which *Salomon* vppon his breast,
In his diuine Pentaculum did weare,
With great *Iehouah* Characters imprest,
That name I loue I reuerence and feare:
That name which *Aron* wore vpon his head,
Grau'd in his holy *Miter* made of Golde,
That name which Angels laude and furies dreade,
Whose praise no tongue can worthily vnfolde,
   That name which flesh is to impure to name,
My sinfull soule with sacred zeale inflame.

                                        Of

Of the Starre which the Magi did worſhip at
Chriſtes Natinitie, and of his death.

I blaze that ſtarre, which was no blazing ſtarre,
But the true figure of eternall life,
The prince of peace was borne then ceaſed warre,
His birthes beginning ended mortall ſtrife,
This glorious ſtarre did lead the aged wiſe
To worſhip th'Infants Godhead in the Eaſt,
Which came with gladſome heart & ioyfull eyes,
To ſee that Babe that made all *Iſraell* bleſt:
O light of Heauen thou waſt extinct on earth,
Yet to our ſoules Celeſtiall life doth giue
Thy death our life, thy riſing our new birth
Thou three daies dead didſt make vs euer liue,
   Yet at thy death obſcur'd was th'earth and ſkie,
   Becauſe he that was God, as man did die.
                     Foun-

FOuntaine of grace from whom doth only runne,
Water of life to saue our soules from death,
O sauiour of the world, pure virgins sonne,
That in red earth infus'd first vitall breath.
Oh thou whose name was calde *Emmanuel*,
Ioyning thy Godhead with humanitie,
Thou that for our sakes didst desc end to hell,
And ouer death did'st get the victorie:
Oh womans seede that didst from God proceede,
By Prophets said to breake the Serpents head,
Thou that in grace and vertue doest exceede,
Content to die that thou mightest quicken deade,
  Thou that didst rayse the dead men frō the tombe.
Earths kingdoms passe, oh let thy kingdome come.
Antient

ANtient of daies, and yet still young in yeares,
Oh God on earthe, Oh man yet most deuine,
Poore in this world, yet chiefe of heauenly Peeres,
Whose glorie in th' infernall pit did shine,
Borne since old *Abrahams* daies yet long before,
(For *Abraham* reioyc'd to see thy daies)
He saw by faith, whom now all powers adore,
The *Cerubins* doe daily sing thy praise,
O God of tymes, and yet in time a man,
Before all times thy time of being was,
And yet in time thy humaine birth beganne,
Least we should fade vntimely like the grasse,
  Oh thou that doest all times beginne and ende,
  Graunt all our workes may to thy glory tende,
                       Of

VVHere liues the man that neuer felt a crosse?
Who Fortunes wheel did neuer tumble down
Where liues the man that neuer suffred losse ?
On whome the starres of heauen did neuer frowne ?
Where liues the man that is in all pointes blest?
Wise valiant, mightie, wealthy, fayre and strong.
If such a one vpon the earth doth rest
His date of life Heauen doth abridge ere long
Such was King *Edward* in his youthfull prime
Who might by *Phœbus* Oracle be deemd
One of the wifest Princes of his time
For wit and learning excellent esteemde
But cruell death maligning his great praise
That in fewe yeares so highly did aspyre
With yron dart misfring'a his golden daies
Whom nations farre away did then admyre
Weeds long time growe, the fayrest flowres do fade
The ripest wits grow rotten at the laft
All thefe faire things which God and Nature made

In

In this huge *Chaos*, ſhall at length lye waſte
Where is king *Salomon* the wiſeſt wight
Of mortall men that liu'd vpon the grounde
Doth he not wander in the ſhades of night,
Whoſe wiſdome through the world was forenound?
What difference betwixt the rich and poore
Irus with *Crœſus* boldly may compare
Both equall are when death ſtandes at the doore
That maketh proudeſt kings like beggars bare,
Then let the wealthy men reſpect their end
Not counting themſelues happy vntyll death,
Sith heauen to them this wealth doth only lende,
Which they muſt pay with loſſe of vitall breath
This made that king of *Lidia* to crye
When he was by king *Cyrus* ouercome:
O *Solon* now thy ſaying true I trie
No man is happie till his day of dome.
That Monarch now is dead that did poſſeſſe,
The golden ſands of bright *Pactolus* waues,
And *Tamberlaine* whom Fortune ſo did bleſſe,

D   That

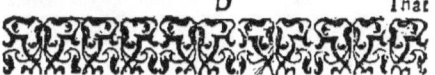

That he a Shepheard made great kings his slaues,
Dead is that mightie king of *Macedon*,
That wept whe of more worlds he hard some talke,
Sith his victorious sword as then had wonne,
Scarce this one world, where we like pilgrims walk
Who being wounded fell vpon one knee,
Fighting against an hoast of barbarous foes,
Said I am mortall by these wounds I see,
For no such bloode from powers Celestiall flowes:
In beautie *Absalon* did farre excell,
Most part of men that sprung of humaine seede,
But when against his Sire he did rebell, (head:
Then heauen did power downe vengeance on his
The sacred scripture truely doth expresse,
That *Sampson* did surpasse all men in strength,
But he that did thowsands in fight distresse,
Was by a womans wiles subdu'd at length,
Beautie is like a faire but fading flower,
Riches are like a bubble in a streame,
Great strength is like a fortefied Towre.

Honoı

Honour is like a vaine but pleaſing dreame,
Wee ſee the fayreſt flowers ſoone fade away,
Bubbles doe quickly vaniſh like the winde,
Strong Towers are rent, and doe in tyme decay;
And dreames are but illuſions of the minde,
Let none puft vp with inſolence deride.
My Fortunes *Autumne* in my prime of yeares,
Sith many diſmall chances do betide,
To royall princes and State-ruling peeres,
I am content with my diſaſter chance,
To follow fate ſith princes lead the daunce;
  Ludit in Humanis diuina pote ntia rebus.
  Et certam praſens vix habet hora fidem.
        D.2

FVNERALL
LAMENTACIONS
VPON THE DEATH OF

his moſt worthy and reuerend vnckle
Maiſter MATHEW EWENS Eſquire one
of her Maieſties Barons of her Highnes Court of Eſchequer.

***

LONDON,
Printed by RICHARD BRADOCKE
for I B.   1598.

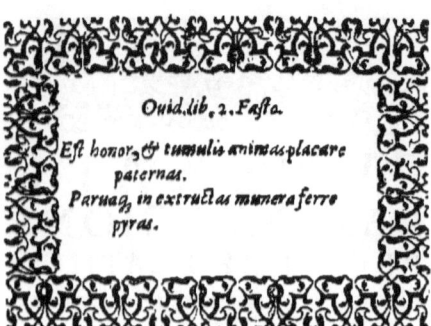

Ouid. lib. 2. Fasto.

Est honor, & tumulis animas placare
paternas.
Paruaq, in extructas munera ferre
pyras.

Funerall lamentations vpon the death
M. Mathevv Evvens *Esquire. &c.*

LET *Numas* death be still deplorde in *Rome,*
Licurgus end let famous *Sparta* waile,
Let *Athens* weepe on *Aristides* toombe,
For there religion lawes and Iustice saile,
But let faire *Cinthias Troynonans* lament,
This Barons death whose flesh returnes to dust,
Whose soule is fled aboue the firmament,
Who liu'd on earth religious, true, and iust.
Now ioye O heauen t'enioy th'earths ornament,
Whose heauenly part to the third heauen is fled
His earthly part to earth doth now relent
Both heauen and earth loue him aliue and dead,
　His flesh to Elements resolu'd doth dye,
　His soule aboue the Element doth flye.
D 4　　　　　　　　　　ſ

QVATORZAIN, 2.

I Know not whether I fhould ioy or weepe
His louing foule doth triumph in the fkie,
But his dead corps in duft a while doth fleepe,
Till heauen fhall ryfe it from mortalitie,
He loft his olde life and hath gaind a newe
Loofing his care he gainde a glorious crowne,
The world loft him, therefore the world doth rue,
He loft the world yet wins for aye renowne,
I loft a friende and therefore I lament,
My friend loft me and I haue loft my felfe
Sith I for his loffe liue in difcontent
He loues heauens ioyes and leaues all worldly pelfe,
  O England now bewaile this fatall croffe,
He loft this world, we gainde a world of loffe.

                                                    He

QVATORZAIN. 3

HE that did feeke the poore mens wrongs to right
  He that maintain'd his natiue countries lawes,
He that in trueth and iuftice did delight
Is now confum'd by deaths deuouring iawes,
Was it by heauens high court of Parliament,
Decreed that his lifes date fo foone fhould ende,
Oh then let vs vpon the earth lament
That we haue loft in him a publique friend
The ioy of many in his graue now lieth,
And he in heauen enioyes immortall bliffe,
His care is vanifht and in him now dieth,
And liues in others that his life doe miffe
    Thus death ftrooke many with this fatall ftroke
    And keeping natures lawes, our lawes He-broke.
                                                Let

QVATORZAIN. 4.

LEt not the world thinke I doe partialize,
  In that I doe extoll my vncles fame,
And striue his glorie to immortalize
By these sad accents which my muse doth frame,
But let men know that he deserues more praise,
Then my poore muse is able to bestow,
Though she doth crown his death with glorious baies
And through the world the breath of fame doth blow
Which breath by multiplying the sweete ayre
May mount the sacred Throne of heauenly powers,
And cause the winged Cherubins repayre,
To mourne his death from their celestiall bowres,
  His vertues merit *Homers* golden pen
  To print his praise with teares of Gods and men.
                                        Let

QVATORZAIN.

Et all men iudge how iuſt a Iudge he was,
  That late was iudged by heauen ſacred doome,
To ſuffer death, that when this life ſhould paſſe
He might obtaine in heauen a glorious roome,
For he among the bleſſed ſaints muſt dwell
Where Patriarches and the Apoſtles ſit,
Which ſhall iudge the twelue Tribes of Iſrael
According as to their deſerts is fit
As here on earth this Iudge was magnifide
Aboue the vulgar ſort in high degree,
In heauen he ſhalbe much more glorifide,
And ſhall enioy the full felicitie,
    And all ſuch Iudges as here iudge aright,
    Shall haue their place in heauē with Angels bright.
                                                        The

QVATORZAIN. 6

THe sacred word doth say thou shalt not kill
  Yet Death thou here doest kill a magistrate;
Dost thou not then infringe Gods holy will
Nor yet the lawes of *Moses* violate?
And wheras mightie kings establish lawes
Thou by thine owne lawe mighty Kings doest slay,
And taking thus away th'efficient cause,
Th'effect, which is the Lawe must needs decay,
Thus now thou takest away a publique guide,
That did mainttine all equitie and right.
Wherefore heauen shall correct thee for thy pride
And shall subdue thy all-flesh-killing might,
  And thou that dost all creatures ouercome,
  Shalt be at last destroyed by heauens iust doome.

If

QVATORZAIN. 7

IF that the soule (as some supposed) might goe,
Out of one bodie to an others brest,
Would that meeke spirit which from him did flow,
In euery Lawyers heart were now imprest
His lifes integritie and zeale was such
He more esteemd of honestie then gold
Which n any now a daies doe loue too much
For loue is oft with money bought and sold,
This rightly may be termde a golden age,
With gold, is fame and reputacion bought
Yet *Salomon* that was most wise and sage,
For wisedome praide, esteming gold as nonght,
  Gold vnto drosse and flesh to dust must turne,
  For this mans losse let the Eschequer mourne.

   Aurea mure vere sunt secula nostrum amor.
   Venit honos, auro conciliatur amor.

                                        Tristia

❡ In obitum Patrui sui colendissimi
Mathei Eueni *illustrissimi Baronis*
Scaccarij *T. R.* nepotis Nænia, siue
carmen funebre.

TRistia Melpomine lachrymarum flumina funde,
   Sit cum perpetuo iunctus amore dolor.
Ille pater patria pollens pietate, Patronus
   Pauperis, & Plebis, per mala fata perit,
Spiritus ascendit splendentis culmen Olympi,
   Diuitias cœli, quas cupiebat, habet.
Non rapuit fiscus, quod non vult Christus habere.
   Non plus quam licuit conciliauit opes.
Ille mihi Patruus charus, patriæ, patriq́;,
   Ergo suus deflet funera mesta nepos.
Doctus erat, facilis natura, mente benignus,
   Moribus humanus, deniq́; morte pius.
Lege Solon, grauitate Cato; sed Tullius ore,
   Nestor consilijs, & pietate Plato.
Membra tegit tumulus, viuit post funera fœlix,
   Fama viget mundo, spiritus astra colit.
Purpureos spargam flores, opobalsama fundam.
   Et plenis manibus lilia pulchra dabo.
His saltem exequijs & munere fungar inani,
   Hic animam donis accumulare velim.

                              Non

Non grates expecto tamen, nec proæmia curo,
  Non hominum laudes: hoc pietatis opus.
Cogit amor patriæ patrie lugere parentem
  Defunctum, tanto debitus urget honos.
O decus, O patria nuper lux, atq; columna
  Natalisq; solis gloria magna vale.
O longum venerande vale, vale, inquit Euene
  Qui tuus est semper fidus amansque Nepos,
Sic viuam & moriar semper tibi certus amicus,
  Musaque cum fatis est moritura tuis
Iurisconsultus, naturæ iure peremptus
  Nunc stabit æterni Iudicis ante Thronum
Qui, vnius homines diuerso iudicet ore,
  Iudex istius Iudicis almus erit.
¡.Sic pia vita fuit, nunc terq; quaterq; beata,
  In rutilo vixit, nobilis vmbra Polo.

F I N I S.

VERTUES DUE.

POWELL'S VERTUES DUE.

THE prefent Tract is printed from an unique and hitherto unknown one. The author was probably the fame Thomas Powell who has verfes before Foorde's (or Ford's) " Fame's Memoriall, or the Earl of Devonfhire deceafed ; with his honourable Life, peacefull End, and folemne Funerall." 4to. Lond. 1606 ; and who wrote alfo the following works :—

Love's Leprofie, 1598.

The Paffionate Poet: with a Defcription of the Thracian Ifmarus, 1601.

A Welch Bayte to fpare Provender, 1603.

Direction for Search of Records, 1622.

The Myfterie of Lending and Borrowing, 1623.

The Attourneys Academy, 1623.

The Attornies Almanacke, 1627.

The Repertorie of Records, 1631.

Tom of all Trades, or the Plaine Path-Way to Preferment, 1631.

Mr. F. J. Furnivall, in reprinting the laft tract among the *Publications of the New Shakfpere Society*, 1876, thus fpeaks of the author. "Our third tract is by a reverencer of Bacon in his diftrefs, a rollicking attorney and Welfhman, Thomas Powell, who feems to have begun writing very bad ferious poetry in 1598 and 1601, and then turnd to chaffing profe,— ftill interfperft with fcraps of bad verfe,—and divers profeffional hand-books, till he ended his career of authorfhip in 1631 with his *Tom of all Trades*, here reprinted. There *may* have been two Thomas Powells. But as the one of 1603—1631 had both a ferious and humorous ftyle in his profe, and in his verfe in his profe-books, I fee no fufficient reafon for fuppofing that he is not the ferious-ftyle verfe-writer of 1598—1601."

Our tract, *Vertues Due*, fully bears out the above character given of fome of his other works by Mr. Furnivall; for, like his firft productions which appeared in 1598 and 1601, this is not only "very bad ferious poetry", but it has a greater fault, that of being in fome places unintelligible. Attempting to foar, obfcurity immediately envelopes him, and to make matters worfe, not content with ufing the hardeft words for the fimpleft fubjects, he preffes into his fervice other words and expreffions not elfewhere to be met with in any work, ancient or modern.

His peculiar temperament feems to render him incapable of telling a plain ftory in a natural manner; and, while ftriving to elevate the verieft common-places into poetical dignity, he makes doubtful what he fhould explain, and by his awkward verbiage and circumlocution fucceeds, not in impreffing his readers with a refpect for his poetical powers, but, with the grave complacency of a Malvolio, in making himfelf a laughing-ftock by his affectations and abfurdities.

Yet fufficient reafons we think may be fhown for the prefent reprint, independent of its rarity; inafmuch as it not only deals with a courtly perfonage, whofe memory has for nearly three centuries been furrounded by a fort of fentimental halo, but as it is the hitherto unknown production of a man whofe other labours with the pen have earned for him a certain degree of notoriety—while, more than all, its remarkable phrafeology entitles it to rank among the minor "Curiofities of Literature."

The Lady herein commemorated was the daughter of Henry Cary, Lord Hunfdon, and firft wife of Charles fecond Baron Howard of Effingham, created Earl of Nottingham, 22 Oct. 1596. He was the celebrated Lord High Admiral, who affifted in defeating the Spanifh Armada in 1588, and who died 14 Dec. 1624 His wife predeceafed him many years, dying at Arundel Houfe, in London, 25 Feb. 1602-3, only a month before Queen Elizabeth, whofe laft days fhe is faid (but on very doubtful authority) to have embittered by her treacherous conduct in not tranfmitting to her fovereign the Earl of Effex's ring, the delivery of which might have been the means of preferving the life of that rafh but ftill-loved favourite. She furvived Effex exactly two years to a day, he having been executed 25 Feb. 1600-1.

She left five children, the third of whom—the eldeft daughter—married Sir Robert Southwell, of Woodrifing, Norfolk, who ferved under his father-in-law againft the Spaniards. The portraits of both thefe naval worthies, it may be mentioned, are given in Pine's engravings from the old tapeftry which was preferved in the Houfe of Lords till its deftruction by the great fire in 1835. Her own portrait and that of her hufband appear in the large painting by Mark Garrard (the property of G. Digby Wingfield Digby, Esq.) in which Queen Elizabeth is reprefented as carried in ftate to Hunfdon Houfe, 18 Sept. 1571. And another full-length portrait of the Earl of Nottingham, painted by Zucchero, is in the Naval Gallery of Greenwich Hofpital.

Vertues due:

Or,

A true modell of the life
of the right Honourable Katharine Howard, late Countesse
of Nottingham, de-
ceased.

By T . P . Gentleman,

Printed at London by Simon Stafford,
dwelling in Hosier lane, neere
Smith-field. 1603.

To the right Honorable,

Charles Howard, Earle of Notting-
ham , Baron of Effingham, Lord high
Admirall of England, of her Maiesties
moſt Honorable priuie Counſayle, and
of the Noble Order of the
Garter, &c.

Ight Noble Lord, my reſolue was
aduiſed, to make immoration vpon
the niceſt circumſtances of your preſent hauiour, in plentifull and honorable ſorrow, whoſe animall motion might bee
admou'd to the violence hereof : This gaue
leaue to the greater obſeruance which wee owe to
the deceaſed, (that is) in protection and conteſta-
tion : Beſides that warrant of the antentique &
Cenſoriall rites, whoſe example I haue here quo-
ted for moſt Honorable Heraldrie, in diſpoſing
her funerall torch by due reference , into your
ſuruiuing hand; neither infeebling the courteſie

A 3   of

The Epistle Dedicatory.

of the liuing, nor promising mine owne aduan-
tage vpon your Noble and innated goodnesse, nei-
ther to actuate, & reiticate molestias, but in
mine owne affectation to be conformed with that
Romane solemnity of dedication,
    And as she was, I write for presidents,
    More of succession, than griefs argument.

Your Honours,

    in all the nerues
    of my ability,

Thomas Powell.

To the Reader.

To prepare ye to what is writ, I know, my ſmootheſt compoſure would be too boyſterous, vpon the rigall nakedneſſe of your impatience. A long preface were a ſicke fether vpon your winged *Mercury*. And yet, to expoſe me to vninſtructed cenſure, whoſe proofe is too much in ſeuerity, I ſhould releaſe the bond of our recōciliation, & ſeeme to ſuſpect approbation, to be more of fortunes almes, than our owne deſeruing. I imply to your freer ſpirits, all cuſtomary requiſites, and to my ſelfe reſerue this onely *obiter* of opinion : That I write more of duty to the dead, than reputation of Iuing Poeſie. In both which, I am wilfully confident, to be confidently willing.

T. P.

Refumptio.

— *Cum tonat Ocyus Ilex,*
Sulphure difcutitur facro quam tuque
domufq́;.

T. P.

Vertues due.

He Sunne but now
began to gather fire,
And lay a sharper edge
vpon his beames,
Abated to the fulnesse
of the yeere,
As fretted with the salt
of Neptunes steames,
When blacke solemnity enuide anew,
And soyld his face with a more precious dewe:

Dew'd with the most religion of affection,
Made soft in nature, and in Heraldry :
The one accusing fate for his election :
The other, weeping his seuerity
  Both from their Cyprus altars offring teares,
  Ynowe to make him aged in yong yeares.

B   It

Vertues due.

It was not for the gods *Arcadian* theft,
When he drew dry their vdders milch-excesse,
Nor for his mother *Pibias*, when she wept
His rage, that earth malign'd his murrinesse.
But, loe, affections law of like for like :
It is our natures freedome to requite.

For he had lustre on his infant rayes,
To blandish out the glory of his Spring,
Reft from the falling Load-starre of our dayes,
Whose motion was the musike which I sing;
The measure of consent to all her sphere :
Indeed she was the best in *Cynthia's* quiere.

She

Vertues due.

She was, (and so are loosers still in leesing,
When they recount the worth of what is lost)
And is not. Cold remembrance euer freezing
When it shall reade the story of what's past.
   Yet as she was, repeate for president
   More of succession, then griefs argument.

Was of her trayne, Eternities decreeing
Did dedicate her in her parentage,
Whose neere alliance askt as neere a beeing,
And gently seal'd it on her virgin waxe:
   And so, for nature and election,
   Would *Cynthia's* selt endeere her as her own.

       She

Vertues due.

She gaue her ranke, reſpect, and full acceſſe,
Agnizing her affinity and merit
With fauours, graces after graciouſneſſe;
Wherein ſhe ſeem'd as if ſhe did inherit
  The truſt and dignities, which long before
  Her Honourable Anceſtors did ſtore.

Her parents honours did ſhe extraduce
Into her very diſpoſition ;
As if the generall *Carey* were infuſde
And had no other formes of his diuiſion,
  Their ancient vnattainted loyalty
  Broad blow'ne, and fluſh vpon her infancy.

Yet

Vertues due.

Yet beauty was not onely of her blood :
Her birth-day *Solstice* height vnto perfection.
The Cantharis enuies a verdant bud,
And birth does only counfaile to protection.
   So learnd fhe with the chãge of euery fpring,
   To faue her blood with heedfull dyeting.

Her youth preferu'd it chafte with continences
A virgin diet for the hote intention,
Which might vngloffe his colour : adde expece,
Both of the length & bredth of their dimefion.
   But the example of her mariage bed,
   Were Oratory to perfwade to wed.

B 3

For

Vertues due.

For after she had blest so many moones,
As had *Astrea*, when she was transfixt;
With more austerity, than that which crownes
The Romane chastity, did she commixe
   Her birth, her blood, Nobility and name,
   To flowe more lofty in as rich veyne:

In *Howards* ample veynes; a Family
Of eminence, deryu'd without distent,
From the first shield of all their Auncestry,
To this of *Charles*, the latest Eminent: (pire,
   Whose fayth and fortunes may they ne're ex-
   But in a melting firmament of fire.

                    She.

Vertues due.

She wedded, yet she was a Votary,
To minister in consecrated flame,
And weare *Dianaes* bow, vpon her thigh,
Till on a day of sanctified name.   (bids,
To store eche Nymph with shafts, the goddesse
To fill her quiuers all with Poplar twigs,

·That grew vpon a leuin, which the sea
Had season'd thriftily within the shores
There *Neptune* fell in loue with *Memone*,
That till this day ne're sawe the Nymph before,
Ne're had his brest improou'd or softened,
But like the temper of his Corall bed:

*V*ertues due.

From which he lately risse to lay her in,
And plac'd his Aggot wreath vpon her browes,
Whose potent charmes *Diana* pardon'd him,
And gaue her back the freedome of her vowes;
　So she might still be of her fayrie trayne,
　He war with *Saturnes* sonnes vpon the mayne.

And now, *Eliza*, with her wedlocke fate,
Did wed her to a higher dignity.
She kept the chayre that did suborne her state,
And grac'd it like the blue-eyde *Cassiope*:
　She ne're surcharg'd ability with grace,
　But still her owne dimensions fild the place :

Wherein,

Vertues due.

Wherein this noble Lady *Katherine* seemd
T'anticipate her Mistris bounteous hand,
As if her offices were but redeemd
From vnder meriting, and she did stand
   Alone, and vnencountred in her worth;
   One whom inheritance had called forth;

Or rather prouidence: for what she was,
She was to others, through her selfe intended :
Like to some interiected leafe of glasse, (ded,
That breaks, yet heats, when neerer rayes offen-
   She was all Organs, euen to the mind,
   Whereby God did insinuate with mankind.

                              Her

Vertues due.

Her whole mortality had this extent,
She had affections of immorrall sense :
For she would pity much, and much relent :
But the affect of greatest presidence
   Ouer her nature, held no sinne to this;
    To leaue apt good vndone, or doo't amisse.

The more they misse of her that are imbayd,
And fortune fixt for want of sea and scope,
Their burden with their sayle being ouerlayd:
Vnlesse they Anchor all their after-hope,
   They misse : alas, I write of that too soone,
    And lend her liuing worth for griefe to come:

                       Yet

Vertues due.

Yet liu'd she to outliue that old report,
Which now againe our new worlds forme: vp-
That, there is no retiremēt in the court, (proue:
Where there is much variety to moue,
   And steale away. O, there's no lif- like hers,
   That liu'd to bury her exceuters.

For softnesse neuer seyz'd her appetite.
A bloodlesse lyuor liues not on his heat:
Her resolution was *Propontick*e right,
And forward stem'd against the Moones retreat.
   No change, no liberty, no ful-eyde pleasure
   Could bring deuotions musike out of mea-
                  (sure,

                              Ie

Vertues due.

It was for her, the million of her sexe,
And calling, doe beside approue their kind;
Whose story often read, as oft begets
Opinion, that the sexe is so inclin'd,
    And calling, so disposed vnto good,
    As well in Courtship, as in woman-hood.

She was a woman, yet, not one of those
Whose erogated heate conuerts to hate.
It was her honour to forgiue her foes,
Euen in their ebbe, and full distent of state.
    Alas, she would not take aduantage than,
    Lest she should trip the fraylty of his man.

She

*V*ertues due.

She would not glory his humility,
Nor actuate her old aggrieuances
O're weake distresse, and present misery :
Such conquest ! O, tis base and honourlesse.
   For when I doe but second Fortunes stroke,
   I wound a heart that is already broke.

She was a Courtier too; but as a Starre
Vnfixt, and like *Orion* in a streame;
As free as featherd Faulcons in the ayre,
Moou'd on no other line, but *Cynthia's* beame :
   Her freer spirit ne're was put in frame,
   Though she put on her selfe a Courtiers name.

                 For

Vertues due.

For she did hospitable bounty too,
And euer kept her influence at home;
Which euery Courtier vses not to doe,
Why, she was nothing Courtier, nor her owne:
Her light was made a Sea-marke to distresse,
Where Fortunes wracks arryu'd their needines.

In Court, no study that would apprehend,
Or aske Religion of her duty more,
Than, what *Eliza* gaue, might still commend
Her most magnificence, and fountayne store:
She was not like a Conduit-pipe fast by,
To turne the streame, & leaue the channel dry.

How

*V*ertues due.

How many feruants of that Royall trayne
Could the freſh image of her loue excite,
To witneſſe, ſhe preferd *Elizaes* fame
Aboue her priuate reputations height!
  She hated to be hyr'de to doe them good,
   Or begd to buy their merits,though ſhe cou'd.

And yet did her contentment ſtretch it ſelfe
More amply: Greatneſſe was aboue her feare;
A faith beyond the curſe that followes wealth,
Who euermore ſuſpects eruptions neere,
Whoſe châge does châge the ſtate of their ſub-
And giues this duty to the next electiõ, (ſectiõ;

                          Great

Vertues due.

Great & secure! Me thinks, tis wōdrous strange:
But gracious not enuyde ! Impossible :
For discontent makes worth his Fret of change,
And not seruility it selfe speakes well
    Of Honourable birth or betterment:
    Respect, with him is feare; & feare, contempt.

I know not how respect came ouer all;
But the most humble did admire her most:
A branch of ranke loue turnd to prodigall:
Such loue is still exhaust, or ouerflowes.
    Ile learne ye how she did diuert their hate:
    She made her selfe as humble as their state.

                                          The

*V*ertues due.

The lyſt of all her vertues had a name
Of greater reuerence,than had the reſt.
Religion. Tis a ſeſsions to arraigne,
Detect,and bring our actions to the teſt.
   And where that liſt was ſlack,remiſſe,& looſe,
   Aſſure ye,it was frailty extraduc'de.

She had no other principles(God wot)
Whereby to leuell and conforme her life:
All was not honeſt that was ſaf-ly got:
She would not by iniuſtice compaſſe right;
   Nor vſde to ſay,Tis *Cæſar* anſweres all;
   So thou reſerue to ſtand, may kingdomes fall.

                    C   Her

Vertues duc.

Her life was but a modell imitation,
Drawne with the freshest colours instance had
In holy writ, which gaue it approbation;
They were her essence (therfore could not fade)
  Like colour layd in wine: her Lenten blacke
  Did sit, like *Nessus* shirt vpon her backe.

At this perfection and maturity,
She stood in natures frayle adoption heere,
When heauen would vouchsafe her first to be
A mother, and her vertues to appeare
  In propagated noblesse of a sonne,
  That layd his roote as far as she begunne,

That

Vertues due.

That first, L. *William* was of *Effingham*,
A Barony, that field and Knighthood earnd
With sweating spurs, when heraldry detaignd
His hardiment. O,'twere a sight to learne,
    And put ambitious fire in any Swayne,
    To see Nobility so dearely gaynd.

Heauen was delighted in his workmanship,
And now became more bountious of his breath,
Which sweld her womb to be more fruitful yet,
Deriu'd a second labors where she left,
    A second blessing, and a *Charter* beside;
    For Honours lofty bed did open wide,

                  C 2   A third

Vertues due.

A third. Inuention, giue me backe, my felfe
Deuided. All my numbers keepe confent,
And with my foule my ftiles ambition melt.
Eche finew of our duty be attent;
    Forget the funerall ftate and maiefty,
    And proftitution wholly fummon me.

Call her by any epithite expreft
In vertues Inuentory; nay difcourfe
Her mothers life : fee with what liuelineffe
She does infert it, freely, and vnforc'd.
    Be fhe the noble Counteffe of *Kildare,*
    Or *Cobhams* Baroneffe; fhee's wondrous faire,

A

Vertues due.

A next. The Lady *Southwel*: here I shou'd
Confound my methode with a plentious vayne
Of great deuotion, and of wyddowhood :
But my more free propofements are reſtraynd,
    To ſhew the loſt, their laſt ſimilitude,
    To which the Lady *Luſon* much accrode.

Here, happineſſe did floate at all the lyne:
This day accounted for the greateſt debt,
That grace and goodeſt Stars could her aſſigne:
And till this day her circle neuer met;
    Now was her happineſſe ſo ſatisfide,   (ſide.
    She knew not what her wiſh might adde be-

              C 3   Content-

Vertues due.

Contentment crownd her streight beyond the
And roughest oppositions in her birth; (mayne,
The weeping *Crocodile*, the *Syrens* strayne,
And all the Delinitions that inuert
    Our, Fye, what ist that we can call our owne?
    She past the seas, & shipwrackt here at home

Within the hauen. Now, it was dispos'd
With heauenly wisdome, to the best of vses.
So, we are wise, to purchase from onr foes,
T'enrich the sea with that which land abuses.
    We doe secure vs in their feebled store.
    Secureneffe hurts least, when it is most poore.

The

*V*ertues due.

The goodneſſe of the Higheſt left her not:
For *Neptune*, conquering *Argo* vnarriu'd,
Muſt diſimbark the golden Fleece ſhe brought,
In her owne hauen to be ſtellifyde,
  And ſeem aboue her weeping Marble ſphere,
  To ſwimme as free in heauen, as ſhe did heere.

'Twas onely in her wiſhes now to dye,
When as her fulneſſe fear'd to be o're-ioyd;
Like thoſe that ſurfet of ſaciety,
And yet their ſurquedry is euer voyd:
  Theſe haue their fulneſſe ſo intemperate,
  Nothing refreſhes, till it ſuffocate.

Vertues due.

She would not haue her Sūmer beames to light
Vpon the rancke, and thrifty slyme beneath,
Where honours heat begets the parasite,
And other monstrous shapes, that wil bequeath
    Vnto their *Cesar*, *Ioues* owne heritance,
    And swell his greatnesse into arrogance.

She fear'd that such shuld know her to be great.
She knew her greatnesse was superlatiue.
Nature, and grace, and stars their rest had set,
And euery opposition left to striue,
    She wanted nothing of felicity,
    But free commission to desist and dye.

                                        She

Vertues due.

She prayd it, and preuented conftant fate,
That would not her delight fhuld fee her fweat
Out of conuerfe familiar, and innate.
I oy, longer then tis frefh, is not compleat :
    But like to Times own tunes, that rauifh not,
    Becaufe they iygd it, when we were begot.

This burthen would be fayne deliuerèd,
When fhe had reckon'd to maturity,
Appealing from the Moone that followed,
The eyght, which mortals call an enemy
    Vnto conception. Fate and fhe complyde,
    And in a feuen-fold happineffe fhe dyde.

The Offering.

Hou that ow'ſt this breathles beau-
Miſtris of the dayes deuotion, (ty,
And her blackeſt rites of duty,
Guyd'ſt her timeles,tuneles motiõ:
    O ! I would not leaue thee yet,
Till I ſee thy Searements fit.

Thou, that art complexion careleſſe,
Let affeƈtions armes vnfold,
After laſt imbracings dureleſſe,
And vpon the hallowedſt mold,
    Lèft for monumentall vſe,
    By thy iuſt extenſure chuſe.

                                   If

Vertues due.

If the earth deny thee reſt,
Like the ſoule that lyes ſo ſoft
In her groning, grieued breſt,
Shalt thou there be buried oft.
    Earth affords no freer Toombe;
    None ſo wide as ſorrowes wombe.

There in ſtead of balmde confeſtion,
Righteous teares, and ſeaſon'd ſighing
Sprinkle o're thy ceaſt complexion,
Till they ſeale thy ſearements plighting.
    Gratefull odours be about thee :
    Truce within, and teares without thee.

Next,

Vertues due.

Next, for Scuchions o're thy herse.
I that truly would display thee,
Offer vp this sacred verse,
VVith the greatest zeale that may be :
  Though thy Herald, length they lacke,
  Yet our Scuchion staues are blacke,

Leafe by leafe, be open wide ;
Speake to all that passe this way,
That they part not from thy side,
Till they read, and reading pray.
  May this story neuer fade,
  Till thy soule be quicke conuayd.

                              Angels

The offering.

Angels with their mufike charmes
All vnknowne malignity;
Drowne the midnights hye allarme,
When the facring fummons be :
   Let not her vnhallowed breath
   Enter in thy houfe of death.

Spirits fanctifide fecure theer
All corruption quite be fpent.
Let thy natures workes affure thee
Confummation imminent.
   Though thou left'ft them all behind thee,
   Yet their merits there refine thee.

Workes

The offering.

Workes and fayth thy foule conuay,
On a heauen-deuiding wing.
Let deuotion reade and pray.
Saints and miniftring Angels fing.
  All, with natures lateft debt,
   Wype away thy Marbles fweat.

FINIS.

LIFE AND DEATH

OF

SIR CHRISTOPHER HATTON.

INTRODUCTION.

TO

PHILLIPS'S COMMEMORATION

ON THE

LIFE AND DEATH OF SIR C. HATTON.

IKE the three preceding tracts, the prefent is areprint of a hitherto
unrecorded work, and of which no other copy is known.

The author, from bearing the fame names, and from poffeff-
ing the fame talent for commemorating great people, feems to be the fame
John Phillips who wrote " Epitaphs " upon the following. I. On " the
Death of the Ladie Maioreffe, late wyfe to the Lorde Alexander Auenet
[more properly Avenon], Lord Maior of London," 1570. II. On " the
Death of Sir William Garrat, chiefe Alderman of the Citie of London,"
1571. III. On " the Death of the Lady Margaret Duglafis good grace,
Countiffe of Linnox," 1578. IV. On " the Death of Lord Henry
Wrifley [Wriothefley], Earle of Southampton," 1581. V. " The Life
and Death of Sir Phillip Sidney," 1587.

All of thefe works are exceffively rare. Truftworthy evidence on
this point is given by the late S. Leigh Sotheby, the eminent book-
auctioneer, who fays, in Jolley's Catalogue, part IV. p. 10, " that he had
no knowledge of the works of a poet named Phillips."

So much has been written about Sir Chriftopher Hatton, and the
romance of his elevation, that it is unneceffary to fay much concerning him
here. The account of his Life by Sir Harris Nicolas collects almoft all that
is known of his public career, but the prefent tract contains fome particulars which were beneath the dignity of a profeffed biographer to record,

even if he were acquainted with them.   The amufing allufions to him and his dancing powers in Gray's "Long Story" and Sheridan's "Critic," will always keep his memory green, when it is forgotten that he was made by his admiring Sovereign, to the aftonifhment of the court, a Lord Chancellor without any knowledge of law.   But an error as to the date of his death is worth noticing for the purpofe of correction.   The true date is 20 Nov., 1591.   Moft biographers print it as 20 Sept., 1591; but among the Burghley "State Papers" is a letter from him to the Earl of Effex, "Lord Generall of her Majefty's Forces in Normandy," dated 5th Oct. in that year.   Eulogiums in rhyme—it is impoffible to dignify them by the name of poetry—of courfe appeared as foon as the needy and expectant verfifiers-by-profeffion could produce them.   The above was, no doubt, the firft one publifhed.   But another was written by the noted Robert Greene, entitled "A Maidens Dreame.   Upon the Death of the right Honorable Sir Chriftopher Hatton, Knight, late Lord Chancelor of England"; which was entered in the Stationers' Regifters, 6th Dec., 1591.   Of this tract only two copies are known to exift—one of which is at Lambeth.

Although Hatton owed his rife entirely to the favour of Elizabeth, who fhowed for him an almoft romantic affection, which lafted many years, and which he reciprocated, at leaft in words, for nothing can exceed the ardour of expreffion in his letters to her (thofe of the Queen to him, unfortunately, have never been difcovered), yet he was, throughout his career, one of the moft painftaking of her public fervants.   He had natural fhrewdnefs and mother-wit, and confiderable aptitude for bufinefs, which ftood him in greater ftead than book-learning.   He was returned to Parliament for Higham-Ferrers, and afterwards having become member for the county of Northampton, he was the organ of Government in the Lower Houfe.   His activity was exhibited in paffing through it the Bill under which Mary Queen of Scots was to be tried, and he fat on the bench as a Commiffioner at the preliminary trials of Babington and the other confpirators.   He was, alfo, one of the Judges for the trial of Mary; and it was by his artful perfuafion that fhe was induced to withdraw her refufal to recognife the authority of the tribunal. It was now that he was created Lord Chancellor; the occupation of which difficult poft, it was thought by his aftute rivals, would effectually prevent him from interfering with their own felfifh plans. How creditably—owing to good management—he filled the office, is well known.

He was not deftined, however, to die a happy or a wealthy man. The Queen, a fhort time before his deceafe, peremptorily infifted—as was her wont in fuch cafes—on his repaying her large fums of money which fhe had provided for the purpofe of his advancement years before. This he was unable fuddenly to do. But her changed conduct, amounting to cruelty, fo affected him that he took to his bed. She then vifited him, and endeavoured to comfort him; but his heart was broken, and he departed this life at the comparatively early age of fifty-two.

The following eulogy of Hatton may not inappropriately clofe this notice. It is extracted from a fcarce work printed in Cambridge, 1595, (which alfo contains one of the earlieft notices of Shakefpeare, as well as references to other contemporary poets), entitled "Polimanteia, or the Meanes lawfull and vnlawfull, to judge of the Fall of a Common-wealth, againft the friuolous and foolifh coniectures of this Age. Whereunto is is added a letter from England to her three Daughters, Cambridge, Oxford, Innes of Court, and to all the reft of her Inhabitants. By W. C." Thefe initials are affigned in the Bodleian Catalogue, 1843, to Wm. Clarke.

"Then name but *Hatton*, the Mufes fauorite: the Churches mufick: Learnings Patron, my once poore Ilands ornament: the Courtiers grace, the Schollars countenance, and the Guardes Captaine. *Thames* I dare auouch wil become teares: the fweeteft perfumes of the Court will bee fad fighes: euerie action fhall accent griefe; honor and eternitie fhall ftriue to make his tombe, and after curious fkill and infinite coft, ingraue this with golden letters, *Minùs merito:* the fainting Hind vntimely chafde [his Creft] fhall trip towards heauen, and *tandem fi* fhall be vertues mot."

Spenfer's Sonnet to Hatton, prefixed to the 'Faerie Queene,' is too well known to require quotation.

HONI·SOIT·QVI·MAL·Y·PENSE

Vt hora, sic fugit vita.

A Commemoration

on the life and death of the right Ho-
nourable, Sir Christopher Hatton,.
Knight, late Lord Chauncellor
of England.

Wherin triumphant Trueth reuiueth his me-
morie from the graue: exhorting Nobilitie, Gen-
trie, and dutifull Subiects, to continue their
obedience to God and her Maiestie, and
to preuent by pollicie the peril-
lous practises of euery ciuil
and forrain enemy.

Published by Iohn Phillips.

Fidenti sperata cedunt.

L O N D O N
Printed for Edward White. 1591.

TO THE RIGHT VVORSHIPFVL
Sir *VVilliam Hatton* Knight, Sonne adopted
and Heire to the right honourable Sir *Chriſtopher Hatton*, late Lord Chaunceller of *England*,
Iohn Phillips wiſheth the feare of
God, cõtinuance of helth,
with increaſe of wor-
ſhip & vertue.

IT hath beene in all times (right worſhipfull) a princi-ciple obſerued, that publick and apparant vertues in per-ſons deceaſed, haue neuer been buried in obliuion, but haue alwaies been recorded and left to poſterities: the end only this, that they who ſtill liue, by apt imitation, might be practi-ſers of like vertues. Which in my ſelfe conſide-red, I concluded, that great vnkindnes to God, and iniurie to remayning Subiects ſhould be offered, if the vertuous life and death of this right hono-rable deceaſed Lord, ſhould not be emblazoned. To God vnkind, if he, as the author, ſhould not be acknowledged, the cauſe efficient of all theſe rich graces, wherewith he was inueſted: & iniurie to ſuruiuing ſubiects, if there ſhould not be comme-

moration

moration of his (more then naturall vertues) as by
recordation whereof, they might walke & tread
the ſame way and path.   My ſelfe I confeſſe, am
the leaſt of others, and moſt vnable to perfourme
what I wiſh, yet wil I not be the laſt that ſhall vſe
endeuour to effect what I may.   (With hoping
that you would accept) I preſumed to thruſt forth
this ſmall Pinnace, fraught with ſimple marchan-
dize, into the harbor of your worſhips protection: aſſuring my ſelfe, that as the pureſt Emerauld
ſhineth brighteſt when it hath no oile, ſo Trueth
will delight you, though baſely apparrelled. The
ſhorteſt and moſt clowdie day, is a day as well as
the longeſt and brighteſt, when the ſun is in the
height of his Horizon.   Pardon then I beeſeech
you, wherein I haue preſumed, and accept (I moſt
humblie craue) what here I haue preſeted: which
if your worſhip vouchſafe, Trueth concludes, her
ſelfe ſufficiently graced, and my ſelfe moſt happy
which haue beene her pen-man. Of this reſting
my ſelfe aſſured, I ſhall continuallie pray for the
increaſe of your worſhip, that both in this
life you may haue your harts deſire,
and in the end, fruition of thoſe
ioyes that are endleſſe.

*Your worſhips moſt duetifull
to cmmaund*

I. Phillips.

A COMMEMORATION OF THE

life and death of Sir *Chriſtopher Hatton*, knight,
Lord Chancellor of England.

YOu noble peeres, my natiue Countrimen,
   I need not ſhew to you my bloud nor birth:
As duſt I was, I turne to duſt agen,
   I go before, but you muſt to the earth.
Yet when, or how, to you it is vnknowne:
For be you ſure the earth doth claime her owne.

It is not gold, nor treaſures that are vaine,
   can you preſerue when that the time is come:
Your houſes gay wherin you do remaine,
   can you not ſhield from Gods decreed doome.
As I am dead, ſo likewiſe you ſhall die:
But learn by death with me to liue on hie.

Though gaping graue incloſe my Corps in clay,
   and ſilent I reſt couered cloſe in mould:
Yet from my ſhrine Trueth ſtriues both night and day,
   to you my mind (good Lords) for to vnfould.
Whereto if caſe you vouch to yeeld regard:
Your ſelues with right, I truſt, wil me reward.

Which of you could with *Hatton* finde a clauſe,
   or ſay that he vniuſt or faithleſſe was?
Did he not liue according to the lawes?
   and on the earth his daies in duetie paſſe?
Was not his care ſet on his God for aye?
And did not he his ſoueraigne Queen obay?

Was not his hart bent for his Countries weale?
   did he not ſtil euen from his tender youth
With rich and poore vpright and iuſtly deale,
   and cloath himſelfe in robes of tried trueth?
If this be true, as no man can denie:
Fame ſaith he liues, although our *Hatton* die.

A 3

Where

Where he might help he would be helping ftill,
    where he might hurt he neuer would do harme:
His chiefeft care was to doe good for ill,
    thus God with grace did gentle *Hatton* arme.
No trecherous thought could harbor in his breft:
The fruites of faith in him were aye expreft.

The worlde knowes wel Trueth tels a tale moft true,
    the heauens aboue of this do witnes beare:
Though *Momus* mates, and *Zoilus* do purfue
    fcandals with fcorne againft the iuft to reare.
But fuch doe weaue themfelues a web of woe:
For Trueth triumphs, who works their ouerthrow.

In luftie youth he lou'd the barbed fteede,
    and *Hector*-like would breake the manly launce:
For martiall acts furnamed *Mars* indeed
    was *Hatton* fweete, that manhood did aduaunce.
At tilt the prize and praife he duely wan:
His might in armes they felt that with him ranne.

At turney he and barriers did excell,
    fome peeres in arms haue borne his battring blowes
In court and towne he was beloued well,
    a fcourge he was vnto his Soueraignes foes.
Faith was the fhield that worthy *Hatton* bare:
Whofe like fcarce liues, his vertues were fo rare.

Should Trueth then dread to fpread his vertues out,
    that for his deedes hath wonne deferued praife?
Her cheareful voice, with courage bold and ftout,
    throughout the world his lafting laud fhall raife.
And moue thereby the minds of noble men
To high attempts, to win them honor then.

Where might the fick, the fore, the halt and blind,
    reape more reliefe then happy *Hatton* gaue?
To fuiters poore he euer was moft kind,
    he fought difpatch that they with Prince might haue
                               Then

Then Lordings learn his ſteddy ſteps to trace:
With God and Prince you thus ſhal purchaſe grace.

Thus for his loue, his faith and tried trueth,
   he of the Guard, by our moſt grations Queene
Was chieftaine made, who firmly held his oath,
   from *Hattons* hart faiths fruites to flow were ſeene.
A chieftaine kind he to the Guard was found:
Whoſe want, with grief their tender harts doth wound

He ſought all meanes to wiſh and work their weale,
   to doe them good he took no ſmall delight:
In their cauſe he with our good Queen did deale,
   t'augment their wage he did all that he might.
From ſixteen pence, to twenty pence a day:
Whil'ſt world doth laſt he did reduce their pay.

And by the day three moneths in the yeare,
   two ſhillings he for them obtaind indeed:
Such feruent loue in him did ſtill appeare,
   that they him found a fort in time of need.
Their wrongs he ſought by ſkil for to redreſſe:
His loue with teares Trueth ſhows they can expreſſe.

In wiſdoms bower he did obtayn his ſeat,
   whoſe lore to learn he did his time imploy:
And God from heauen with his graces moſt great,
   in mercies milde ſought to augment his ioy.
For vertues vſe wherein he took delight:
Our gratious Queen did dub our *Hatton* knight.

Diſcreet he was, and wary in his wayes,
   raſhly to ſpeak at no time he thought fit:
In faith and feare he ſpent his Pilgrims dayes,
   for common weale he did imploy his wit.
Where *Syno* ſought his treaſons to inure:
His cenſures graue conuinced the impure.

And as from Trueth at no time he did erre,
                     but

but truely fought the Trueth for to vphold:
He had a care his feruants to preferre,
   the good found grace, the wicked he controld.
The poore oppreft he wifely did defend:
And on the poore a portion he did fpend.

Belou'd of all he was for vertues vfe,
   the grafts of grace in *Hattons* breft did grow:
By wifdoms lore he brideled all abufe,
   and did himfelf a loyall Subiect fhow.
Thus he with God did grace and fauour find:
Whofe facred trueth he planted in his mind.

And with our Queen that princely Phenix rare,
   whofe like on earth hath fildome times bin feen,
He was efteemd and fet by for his care,
   as noble Peeres that aie haue trufty been.
Vizcechamberlain her Highneffe *Hatton* made:
Whofe tried trueth could neuer faile ne fade.

The curfed curres of *Catalin* vnkind,
   that did confpire againft her Royall Grace:
And to fubuert the State did beare in mind,
   with might and maine he fought for to difplace.
Thofe wily Wolues vntrufty to the Crown:
By Iuftice he threw topfie turuie down.

Our princely Queen whome God from danger faue,
   of Counfaile hirs, did *Hatton* fure elect:
Who *Solon*-like did vfe his cenfures graue,
   the good to fhield, the wicked to correct.
And as he was adornd with graces great:
So fate he fafe in honors blisfull feate.

Lord Chanceler then her Grace did him ordaine,
   Which charge with care he wifely did difcharge,
For fuccour fweet none came to him in vaine,
   good confcience had her fcope to goe at large.
The right of might need not to ftand in awe:
Ne would he trueth fhould be defaft by lawe.

Affection could in *Hatton* beare no fway,
No giftes nor gold might once corrupt his minde:
Fraude to fubuert, he ftudied night and day,
To equitie his heart was aye enclinde.
   Where confcience was corrupt and found vncleane,
   to vanquifh he, by wifedome fought the meane.

Oppreffed men from daunger he did fhielde,
Their wofull wronges he wifely did redreffe;
In deepe difpaire fweete comfort hee did yeelde,
To eafe their griefe that languifht in diftreffe.
   And where as Trueth durft fcarcely fhewe her face,
   Fraude was fubdude, and foyled with difgrace.

The Lawes he fought, with confcience for to vfe,
Triumphant Trueth, he feated in her throne:
To heare the poore he neuer did refufe,
Right glad he was to helpe them to their owne.
   Wrongs went to wracke, Craft could no harbour finde,
   To maintain trueth our *Hatton* was enclinde.

Thus Lordings all his life you may beholde,
That liuing heare hath wonne deferued fame:
And though his corps lye couered clofe in molde,
In Court and towne fhall liue his fpotleffe name.
   Death dies in him, his vertues death hath flaine,
   And hee by death eternall life dooth gaine.

Yet from his graue, Trueth dooth you all exhort,
To lincke your hearts and mindes in loyall loue:
Let faith in you builde fuch a famous fort,
That nothing may from trueth your mindes remooue.
   Though Pope and Spaine, againft your peace doe iarre,
   Withftand their rage, prepare your your felues to warre.

Clap Corflets on, your ftanderds take in hande,
Your barbed fteedes beftride with courage ftoute:
Brandifh your fwordes, fight for your natiue lande,
By Seas and fhores befet your foes about.
   Nowe is the time where honour may be founde.
         B   Thinke

Thinke on the acts, your Aunceftours haue doone.

Hafte to your fhippes, hoyfe failes in name of God,
Man you your coaft, march after warlike Drumme:
Your Enfignes braue, each where difplay abroade,
Downe with your foes, that for your fpoyles doe come.
 Take Lyons hearts, feare not your hatefull foes;
 But let them feele, your manly battering blowes.

They come to facke, your Citties, Fortes, and Towres,
Your Wiues and maides they purpofe to deflowre:
Stande to it then, and cracke thofe crakers crownes,
That thinke to win your wealth, within an howre.
 Be bolde in God, and neuer turne your backes,
 But beard thofe braues, that mind to worke your wracks.

You are, and haue beene feared ouer all,
England's an Ile, of ftoute and hardie men:
Be ftronge in faith, your foes downe right fhall fall,
For one of you, in armes fhall vanquifh ten.
 You fight for God, and God your guide fhall be,
 And from the handes of enemies fet you free.

Richard the firft, of England famous King,
Good Lordings vouch, to call vnto your minde:
Whofe Martiall acts, throughout the World dooth ring.
The Heathen rout, of Pagans moft vnkinde
 His force haue felt; whofe manly conquering hand,
 No Pagan proud was able to withftand.

And then fhall Spayne, a fincke of deadly finne,
Or raging Rome, a cage of Birdes vncleane:
Be bane of you and yours, as they beginne?
Or from your heads, the creft of glorie gleane.
 As yerft of yore, plucke vp thofe rotten weedes ;
 Let heauen and earth, record thofe conquering deedes.

Edward the third, your King of rich renowne,
Againft the French did vfe his conquering fworde:
Mauger their beardes, he did poffeffe their Crowne,
           The

The French were faine, to ferue him as their Lord.
  Take courage then, maintaine your Countries right,
  Gainft *Rabfica*, in Gods name enter fight.

Henry the fift, I wifh you not forget,
At Agent Court, thinke what a field he fought:
When all the powre of Fraunce him round befet,
Ten thoufand men, them to fubie&ion brought.
  Though night before, they Bonfires great did make,
  And made their boaftes, what prifoners they would take.

But they that bragge of conqueft and renowne,
Before the fielde be fought, or truft their ftrength:
We fee the Lord in moment can caft downe,
And giue the weak'ft the vi&orie at length.
  Though Englands King, and his, they bought and folde,
  The French were flaine, though they to brag were bold.

Then though to Spaine, the Pope haue giuen your land,
And your good Queene depofed from her Crowne :
A conqueft win, your weapons take in hand,
The pelting pope, and Spaniards proude beate downe.
  As earft to fore, you Conquerers haue beene
  Through world, now let, your cõquering deedes be feene.

What Nation yet, that menac'ft you with warre,
But you haue met, and giuen the vtter foile :
Snaffle thofe Coultes, that at your peace doe iarre,
And beard thofe braues that labour for your fpoile.
  Fight for your felues, your wiues and Children now,
  To ftraungers Yoakes, your neckes doe neuer bow.

Thus Trueth her charge, to rich and poore hath tolde,
From this good Lord, whofe life to you is knowne:
And Trueth to you fuch tydings will vnfolde,
As may enforce both yonge and olde to moane.
  Marke *Hattons* ende, whom death from vs hath reft,
  Yet *he* good name to conquer death hath left.

Thus as in health, in trueth he God did praife,

In ſickenes his, he did extoll his name,
His hope was heauen, by faith on Chriſt he ſtaies,
And battaile dooth gainſt ſinne and hell proclaime.
    Rebelling fleſh he manly did ſubdue,
    And in ſweete Chriſt his health he did renue.

Moſt like a Lambe amidſt his greeuous paine,
He beares the Croſſe that God vpon him laide:
With patience hee his anguiſhes ſuſtaines,
In extreamſt griefe moſt faithfully he praide.
    Chriſt was the rocke, whereon he ſought to builde,
    All other meanes this Chriſtian Lord exilde.

Thus in Gods trueth his heart and minde was ſtaide,
He ſtudied ſtill to exerciſe his Lawe :
By-pathes to treade he euer was affraide,
Of iudgement he did alwaies ſtande in awe.
    His Lord and God, right glad hee was to ſerue,
    He from his heaſts, of purpoſe would not ſwerue.

Thus ſpent this Lord his time in his diſtreſſe,
On Gods ſweete will he alwaies did depende:
To handfaſt Chriſt by faith he foorth did preaſe,
And he through grace, did ſweete releife him ſende.
    Though bodie his, were feeble, faint, and weake ;
    His ſoule was ſtrong, Chriſt kept the ſame from wreake.

When phiſicke ſought, his health for to recure,
He held Gods word the phiſicke for the Spirite :
From thence he dranke ſuch precious water pure,
As in the heauens augmented his delight.
    Yet phiſicke ſhew'd on him her wonted skill,
    But all in vaine, for God muſt haue his will.

Our gratious Queene, of curteſie the flowre,
Faire Englands Gem: of laſting bliſſe and ioye:
Whom God long ſhielde with arme of might and powre,
From all her foes that would worke her annoye.
    From *Rich mount* came, this Lord for to releeue;
    Whoſe Princely ſight great comfort did him giue.
                              All

All meanes fhe fought to worke her *Hattons* eafe,
Moft louing wordes fhe gaue the ficke and weake:
Her Highnes voice his griefes did much appeafe,
His heat reuiu'de to heare her Highneffe fpeake.
    Phifitions then, had charge to fhewe their skill
    Vpon this Lord, as they would win good will.

And they with care, (as fubiects to her Grace)
Obedient were, to waite vpon their cure:
On whom they wrought, God knowes a certaine fpace,
Deuifing howe, their health he might procure.
    Fiue daies our Queene remain'd with the deftreft,
    Who thought himfelfe through her for to be bleft.

She tooke her leaue and bad this Lord farewell,
And he to heauen with handes outftretched hie:
Calles vnto him, that in the heauens dooth dwell,
With grace from heauen her Highnes to fupplie.
    Long liue faide he, moft gratious Queene in peace,
    God make thee ftronge, the rage of foes to ceafe.

Thus praide our Queene to God to fende him health,
And he to heauen for her fafegard dooth call:
That long fhe might liue in the common wealth,
To fhield the good and bring the bad to thrall.
    He tooke his leaue of his moft gratious Queene,
    And praifed God fhe had his comfort beene.

Phifitions then did on this Lord attend,
And graue diuines were euer at his hand:
But that which God dooth minde to bring to end,
Its vaine for man to gain fay or withftand.
    His hope was heauen, his truft was in Gods fonne;
    Small was the eafe, that he by phificke wonne.

Time paffeth on, and calles this Lord away,
The Sexten waights to ring his dolefull Knell:
But he prepares himfelfe to watch and pray,
He leaues the world, and hopes with Chrift to dwell.
    And as by Chrift in trueth this Lord was taught,

With

With th'oyle of faith his Lampe was fully fraught.

Securely *he*, to fleepe thought it not meete,
The fleepe of finne, *he* did abandon quite:
He look't for Chrift, *His* Lord and Sauiour fweete,
His hope and truft in his deere death was pight.
   His wedding Roabes with ioy he did prouide,
   In hope to feaft with Chrift and his fweete Bride.

What were the words he to the world did leaue?
He by his will all things in order fet:
He fought no man of duetie to deceiue;
His hope was Chrift, from him he comfort fet.
   And as he had beene euerie poore mans friend,
   So he in minde the poore had to his end.

The Schooles of fkill, where fcience dooth abound,
He thought vppon: and dayly had in minde
Poore Captiues that in clogs of care are bound,
To eafe their griefe he fome releife affignde.
   His feruants all, whofe loue to him was tender,
   For feruice doone, he duely did remember.

But waxing faint, and drawing to his ende,
He leaues his Queene vnto the Lord of might:
Defiring him, from griefe her to defende;
And all her foes to foile and put to flight,
   From treafons vilde, and Traytors, Lord her faue,
   And let thy Trueth, through world her paffage haue.

Farewell my Peeres, the Lord God be your guide,
Her Counfell graunt, with thy grace to direct:
That they a falue may day by day prouide,
To fhielde the good, and cut off the infect.
   Her Highnes weale, God make them ftill to minde,
   And to roote vp rebellious plants vnkinde.

You manly Knights and Gentlemen adue,
Be ftronge in Trueth, and conftant to your Queene:
Farewell to you good Subiects iuft and true,
                       Nowe

Nowe from your hearts let loyaltie be feene.
    Vpholde the ftate, be Pillers found of truft:
    Falfe not your fayth, to God and Prince be iuft.

Be not feduc'ft, by any popifh meane;
Abhorre and hate their doctrine moft vnpure:
Thofe rafkall Priefts, as Traitors holde vncleane,
That would you from obeyfance due allure.
    Cleaue you to Chrift, let Pope and blind guides goe,
    They fpeake of peace, but minde your ouerthrowe.

Thus time in Trueth runne ouer faft away,
And fickenes fharpe gaue more and more increafe:
And death dooth waite, to clofe his corpes in clay,
But he for grace, to call dooth neuer ceafe.
    Sweete Chrift I fue, for mercie vnto thee;
    Bowe downe thine eare, from hell my foule fet free.

His fonne adopt, Sir *William Hatton* Knight,
He dooth exhort obediently to liue:
In God and Trueth he wils him to delight,
And to his Prince her honour due to giue.
    Thus fhalt thou win deferued praife and fame,
    And fpotleffe keepe for euer *Hattons* name.

And thankes to you my Seruants for your paine,
Hencefoorth for mee you may take eafe and reft:
I fee with you I fhall not long remaine,
For death to facke my life is prefent preft.
    But pray my faith in Chrift may neuer faile,
    Life is no loffe, death workes for mine auaile.

And now fweete death moft welcome vnto mee,
Thy ftroakes ne can, ne fhall me once difmay:
No griefe but ioy, I fhall obtaine by thee,
Although thou come to take my life away.
    Yet Chrift to me a Crowne of life will giue,
    Death dies in his, and his with him fhall liue.

I call to thee, O Chrift my Sauiour come,
                        My

My filly foule into thy bofome take:
And in the great and dreadfull day of doome,
A member of thy kingdome Lord me make.
 I come to thee; thy Seruaunt Lord receiue,
 My corps to clay, my foule to thee I leaue.

O happie Lord that made fo good an end,
Thy Queene thy want, with noble Peeres dooth waile:
Thy fonne adopt, laments his deereft friend,
Drie dumpes of dole, conftraines his ioy to faile.
 Poore Suters weepe, thy feruants penfiue are;
 The needie poore with teares, their woes declare.

Thus Trueth the trueth hath fet before your eyes,
His life and death moft truely is fet downe:
And let the trueth both rich and poore fuffice,
Who fpreades his praife, in euery Port and Towne.
 A godly life he ledde vpon the earth,
 And in Gods feare did render vp his breath.

Then Lordings yeelde in weedes of wailefull woe,
To bring his corps vnto the gaping graue:
Hee's gone before, the way he dooth you fhowe,
And you your felues of life no charter haue.
 Then thinke on death, which way fo ere you wend,
 He followes you, your pilgrimage to ende.

Thus though this Lord vnto the world be dead,
His faith in Chrift the ioyes of heauen hath wonne:
Sinne, Hell, and Death, he vnder feete dooth treade,
And liues in bliffe, with Chrift; Gods onely fonne.
 Then Lordings chaunge your griefes to ioye againe,
 For *Hatton* liues and death in him is flaine.

FINIS.

www.ingramcontent.com/pod-product-compliance
Lightning Source LLC
Chambersburg PA
CBHW020116030726
47498CB00006B/2126